M000158318

PLAYING
WITH FIRE

Also by Alison Tyler

A Is for Amour
Afternoon Delight
B Is for Bondage
Best Bondage Erotica
Best Bondage Erotica, Volume 2
C Is for Coeds
Caught Looking (with Rachel Kramer Bussel)
D Is for Dress-Up
E Is for Exotic
Exposed
F Is for Fetish
Frenzy
G Is for Games
Got a Minute?
H Is for Hardcore
Hide and Seek (with Rachel Kramer Bussel)
Hurts So Good
The Happy Birthday Book of Erotica
Heat Wave
I Is for Indecent
J Is for Jealousy
K Is for Kinky
L Is for Leather
Love at First Sting
Luscious
The Merry Xxxmas Book of Erotica
Naughty or Nice
Never Have the Same Sex Twice
Open for Business
Red Hot Erotica
Slave to Love
Three-way

PLAYING
WITH FIRE

EDITED BY
ALISON TYLER

Copyright © 2009 by Alison Tyler.

All rights reserved. Except for brief passages quoted in newspaper, magazine, radio, or television reviews, no part of this book may be reproduced in any form or by any means, electronic or mechanical, including photocopying or recording, or by information storage or retrieval system, without permission in writing from the publisher.

Published in the United States by Cleis Press Inc., P.O. Box 14697, San Francisco, California 94114.

Printed in the United States.
Cover design: Scott Idleman
Cover photograph: Christine Kessler
Text design: Frank Wiedemann
Cleis Press logo art: Juana Alicia
First Edition.
10 9 8 7 6 5 4 3 2 1

For SAM

Water, water I desire,
Here's a house of flesh on fire;
Ope' the fountains and the springs,
And come all to bucketings...

—Robert Herrick

Contents

INTRODUCTION:
LIGHT MY FIRE

I don't have to tell you that I'm the type of girl to hold my hand over a flame. I don't have to confess that the glow in a man's eyes over a lit match makes me wet. And I don't have to whisper to you that I have an undeniable urge to move closer to incendiary situations, when I ought to flee in the other direction.

But I am telling you.

I'm telling you that danger doesn't just turn me on.

It lights my fire.

In this collection of twenty-one erotic stories, couples set their boundaries aflame, like in Shanna Germain's "White Heat, White Light":

> *Despite her stare, I take his cigarette. I take it and slide it into my mouth to taste the spongy paper that is supposed to filter, to protect me from something: the smoke, the heat; myself.*

Sommer Marsden's "Fire Woman" focuses on a different type of warmth:

*Buried deep inside her heat, I had fucked her until
I thought my vision was going, bright white spots
appearing in my sight in the murky purple light.*

While A. D. R. Forte's "Texas Hot" is all about the weather:

*Heat-soaked air, moist and sticky like my fingers on
my clit as I watch him from my window: Shirtless,
denim shorts. Skin glistening with sweat.*

See, there's hot and then there's *hot*. Some writers poured out the
emotional kerosene and tossed on a match. Others watched the
temperatures rise indoors and out. One creative author wooed
me with a water tale, which I used to end the book—a cool
refreshing finale to a crackling collection.

Be it a flick of a BiC or the glowing embers of a bonfire, these
stories will stoke anyone's fire.

XXX,
Alison Tyler

LUCIFER
AND VENUS

Nikki Magennis

When I think of him I smell the hot gravel tang of phosphorus.

He lights matches with his thumbnail. He'll burn a whole box, flicking each red-tipped head until it flares into life, shaking out the brief flame and tossing the blackened stick at his feet. Profligate. Fickle. Mesmerizing.

Every night he circles, restless, glittering at every woman he passes. And later still, when the night's bleaching pale, at last he'll drag that sharp nail across my throat, between my breasts, over my belly, and down to the soft dark shadows.

He'll strum until I catch light and turn brilliant.

> Venus ("The morning star") used to be called Lucifer as it rose in the morning "like a second sun."
> — Pliny the Elder, *Historia Naturalis*

"Lucifer," or light-bringer, was also a term used for early friction matches.

FIRE WOMAN

Sommer Marsden

Emma likes to watch the fires. The ones we set for rookies so they can practice. She sits back on the perimeter so the chief doesn't catch her and she paints herself. The first time I saw her doing that, I thought she was doodling on her skin. Instead she was painting her smooth tan skin with invisible ink some bouncer named Mac had given her.

That first time, I tried not to be distracted with her sitting out in the high weeds. She sat in a canvas camping chair like she was at a baseball game. Her hair, the same color as wheat in the fall, whipped in the high wind—the same wind that was driving the flames to dangerous heights. I was watching her when I should have been watching Brian, the new kid. My gaze kept pulling to her way out there, hunched forward like she was about to cheer. Then she would look down and write on herself with that pen that looked like a kid's magic marker.

"Little attention here, Zach!" the chief called, and I yanked myself back into the moment. Gustafson is a really nice guy and following my gaze, he said, "Anyone gets hurt and her ass is out of here, got it? I know you have yourself a little firebug. That's cool as long as this is the extent of it, but I can't have anyone getting hurt because your dick's got you distracted."

I nodded. "Got it. No problem." I stopped watching her but in the back of my mind, I couldn't help but wonder about what she was writing. I found out. And my dick was happy.

Now we're out in the sun, and it's about a hundred in the shade. Emma's in her cutoff sweat shorts that should be illegal and a tank top. Her honey blonde hair is tugged up into a messy knot that almost makes it look as if she's been electrocuted.

"You're fucking up the hose, Nelson," I bellow and my eyes go to her on their own. She's writing again. And responding to the stimulus like Pavlov's dog, my cock grows rigid and my pulse amps up. The hot humid air becomes even heavier as I try to draw it into my lungs.

I glance back in time to see Nelson right his wrong and I yell, "There you go. Keep it straight!" so the captain will know I am paying attention and not daydreaming about fucking Emma up the ass like two weeks ago when she had written little instructions along her skin. Then she had taken me home and turned on her black light. I had followed the instructions explicitly, reading her creamy tanned skin as it glowed neon white in the odd heavy light.

Eat my pussy…had been written above the waistband of her shorts. I had followed that order with glee until she squirmed, thighs clamped around my head, and moaned about how my stubble rubbed and hurt but felt so good. She came for me then, sweetness sliding over my lips and my tongue, three fingers buried in her sweet cunt.

Fuck me doggie style…had been written on one thigh.

And I had flipped her over, giving her tight little ass about six good smacks. I alternated the way she liked until her back arched and her head flew back. I pressed my cock to her and slid in with one agonizingly slow stroke. Buried deep inside her heat, I had fucked her until I thought my vision was going, bright white spots appearing in my sight in the murky purple light.

I had reached around to rub her clit until she flexed under me, thin but strong, the muscles in her back bowing with the force of her orgasm.

"Read my right calf," she had gasped, and I had glanced down to see it. I'd almost come right there. Right then.

Fuck me up the ass, Zach...the impossibly greenish white letters had read and I felt my cock jerk involuntarily. I had made some deep caveman sound and she had said, in a voice full of knowing, "Lube's under my pillow."

We used nearly all of it. Until she was coated in the cool slick gel and I was slicked up and so slippery handling my own cock had been like handling a wet eel. When I pressed to her and she pressed back, I'd nearly lost it again. But after two false starts, I had buried myself in the hot tightness of her ass and in six glorious strokes had come like I was dying.

I pull my attention back to Nelson, who has now stumbled and somehow in the heavy gear, with the heavy hose, strapped himself under the monstrosity. I run ahead and whip it to the side so he can roll out. "Cap sees you and you're fucked. No time for rolling around on the ground when the fucking house is on fire," I say, a little more harshly than I intend.

Just then a yellow orange tongue of flames licks at the hot blue summer sky and I see Emma in my peripheral vision. Her head is thrown back like in orgasm, her eyes wide when she pushes her sunglasses back. Her hair whipping in the hot dry wind. She squirms like she is wet between her legs and my cock jerks again—wanting her and what she has. The feel of her, the heat of her, the little sounds she makes when she comes that make me fucking crazy. In my mind I hear the song I always sing to her, *T-t-t-t-twistin like a flame in a slow dance, baby. You're driving me crazy. Come on, little honey. Come on now...*

But we barrel on, Nelson and I and the other guys on duty today, the other ones who are sweating and panting and ready to die to teach a handful of rookies how to keep other people from dying. But in my mind, I'm fucking Emma in the black light.

When my shift is done, she's sitting in the SUV with the engine running. The inside is cool and her sweat shorts have bunched up and show the tops of her smooth thighs. I can see the swell of her pussy lips because she isn't wearing panties. The tinted windows give the inside of the vehicle a secret cave feel.

"Get in the back," she says, shifting in her seat in that urgent way that instantly gets me hard.

I climb between the seats, shoving my bulk through the too small opening. The back seats are down. I hadn't noticed. I hear the power locks engage and then she is backing through the opening, her ass coming at me in her super-short shorts. I put my fingers up under the ragged hem and touch her ass, find her slick heat, finger her as she tries to maneuver, a low laugh escaping her.

"You have no patience."

"True." I yank her back to me and push at her shorts. "God, I want to fuck you."

She hands me something small and black. Made of smooth plastic, it fits in my hand. "What is it?"

"Thumb the button." She kisses my lower lip and runs her small hand over the ridge of my cock. My Dickies are filthy and harsh with dust. They rasp under her touch. She squeezes and a warm slow pleasure takes me over.

The black light springs to life, and the inside of the car is now a nightclub. I can only assume this is on loan from the infamous Mac. She turns and smiles, her white teeth glowing like the Cheshire cat's in *Alice in Wonderland*. I do feel like I've fallen down the rabbit hole, but I like it very much. Along her cleavage she has written, *Unzip your pants. Show me your cock...*

"Well," she says. "What are you waiting for?"

I do as instructed and stare transfixed as my cock springs free and aims right at her. It's got a mind of its own, or so it seems. She leans forward, on hands and knees. A gorgeous creature with wild hair and a wilder nature. She takes me between her lips and her teeth glow surreally as she sucks me in. I watch my hands as I shove them into her mass of hair, watch the white nails shine like phantoms as they disappear to burrow in the honey-colored mess. "Oh, god."

"Your cock is hot. Really hot." She licks up the back and then swallows me down. I clench my jaw to stave off the orgasm that is rocketing toward me.

She sucks and licks until I'm fucking her mouth like I have no manners at all. But she likes it. She always has. And that leaves me free to fuck hard and pull her hair a bit. She pushes me back and lifts her top to bare her midriff.

*Ride him cowgirl...*glows along her flat belly. I can't help but laugh as my cock points straight up in the small dim back of the SUV. She climbs aboard, the inside of her unbelievably hot, hotter than the burning building I have just left. Emma leans in, kisses me, bites my lip.

"This won't take long," she says. "I want you so bad. But don't come, Zach, don't come, okay?"

I nod, grit my teeth, pray I can keep my word as she starts to move.

The small light has lit the inside of the car and I watch bits and pieces of her body, her skin, her clothes flashing like sunlight off of water. When she tosses her head back and cries out as she comes, her cunt clenching around me so tight it nearly hurts, I pinch her nipples and she makes a lower noise that almost pushes me past my ability to hold fast.

"I don't think I'm good for much longer, Em," I manage.

She slides down me and she's humming. "I like to watch you with the fire," she says. Her tongue drags along my thigh; her teeth flash surreal and bright.

"I know, baby." I'm touching her hair again.

"I like to smell the smoke on you," she says and licks along my shaft until I have to shut my eyes.

"I know, baby." It is a smell that most women hate.

"I like how hot you are when you walk through the fire," she says and swallows me whole. I feel like I'm all the way down her throat and her tongue is dancing over me and I am turning into smoke and flames and bright fairy lights that glow like the sun.

"I know, baby. God, I know." And I am coming, clutching at her hair.

WHITE HEAT, WHITE LIGHT

Shanna Germain

Night is falling. In the rising dark, I am free. For now. The bonfire lights my way to him, a grounded star trail a thousand hours long. I travel with the speed of light on winged sandals until I am there, in front of him, fierce and free in my summer dress. In the wind, my hair whips around my head. It makes untamable snakes with pretty patterns.

He notices. We've noticed each other all day, with the kind of noticing that happens in the eyes and the mouth and the body. The kind of noticing that is only noticed by the people doing it. Or so we'd like to believe. Now, we drift toward each other around the bonfire, pretending this is not a predestined course. Pretending this orbit does not end in collision.

From here, with the bonfire so close, with him so close, I look back and barely see the light that shines from the window of my cabin. Inside that cabin, there is a man sleeping. I won't think about him. Instead, I'll look into the face of this other man, the one who stands in front of me now, holding out a cigarette.

I don't smoke, but I take the cigarette from his fingers. He has blue eyes, the kind of blue that I'll see in the crash of waves a hundred years from now and that will knock me to my knees. I know this, like I know what sadness is coming on the blue dawn. What pain.

It doesn't matter now. In the dark, the blue dawn is a thousand hours away. First, there is this bonfire, big as a horse, a house, a barn, burning down the sky. In the middle of nowhere, lake on one side, forest on the other, the fire is the only thing bright enough to scare away the stars. As it grows, more stars blink out. The tiny Dolphin has already disappeared in the dark sea of sky. Part of the Eagle's wing has folded from sight. From her black bedspread, the chained lady—Andromeda—watches still, her bright stars glittery as eyes.

Despite her stare, I take his cigarette. I take it and slide it into my mouth to taste the spongy paper that is supposed to filter, to protect me from something: the smoke, the heat; myself.

My dress is too flimsy for the night. The fire licks at it with its heated tongues but doesn't come close enough to warm me. I slide closer to him, let his silhouette cover me like a blanket.

The wind picks up, gathers sand and sparks and grinds them together in small whirlwinds that grit my eyes. I can't close them. I'd miss something in the far reaches of his eyes, in the hidden corners of his fingers. Is this how Andromeda feels? I wonder. Destined to see all, to watch forever, even as her eyes thunder and bring rain.

"Want me to light it for you?" he asks. I do. Of course I do. He doesn't lean in with a lighter or cup his hands around a match. He slides the cigarette from the stickiness of my lips. I taste the smoke of the night. Filter gone. Protection gone. Gone.

His mouth opens to the cigarette showing tongue and teeth, his lips against the yellow filter. I hear the *click-click* of the silver lighter opening, the flick of the flame, that suck and hiss of tobacco and paper catching the light. In the flare, his blue eyes spark with yellow.

When he hands the cigarette back to me, the end tastes like him, like what I'm hoping he tastes like: marshmallows burnt on the outside. No, like licking the stick the marshmallows were burnt on. Crisp and brutal and dark on the outside, the bright green of youth underneath. Bendable. Not something I can break.

I inhale.

He carries his wallet on a chain. I saw it earlier, the metal loops that swing from belt to pocket. It's his secret rough-and-tumble, the only part of him that isn't clean cut. When he moves, it clinks together.

He bends his head to light his own cigarette, the end another small star that flickers between us. *Click,* the lighter closes.

"Want to walk?" he asks. It's not what he's saying, but that's what comes out. "Get away from all—"

"Yes."

It isn't until we step out of the circle of the fire, toward the dark trees that look not like trees, but like a wall, a tall dark wall with only one way in and no way out, that I realize how many people are around the bonfire. All of them doing the same things: Lighting their smokes. Drinking. Making choices that draw the dawn closer or push it away. Time travel. I'd forgotten all of them, busy trying to close the distance between his eyes and mine, trying to open it up. Space travel.

Their voices carry as we slip away. Laughter and tales of shared experiences. The sharing of new experiences. Storytelling, ancient, revered. That is enough for so many. My story's been told: Vanity. Infidelity. Infinite. That old, old tale. It is time to start again. A new telling.

We walk. Somewhere between here and there, we leave the light of the fire and join the dark shine of the stars, the red-cherry end of our cigarettes. The trees are close enough that I can reach my hand out and feel them stirring. This one's dark bark makes riverbeds beneath my fingers.

My smoke is smoked, my head is swimming, but I don't want to let it go. I suck the filter. There's that taste again. Him. I hope. He takes it from me, pushes both cigarettes out at once on the bark.

"You know what you're doing to me? What you've done?"

I could say no, but it wouldn't be fair. It wouldn't be true. There will be no truth come the blue-dawn morning, so the time for truth is now, in his blue-eyed night.

"Yes," I say. "I know." This boast, this brag of beauty: it is all I have. The lake looked into me all day and I know I cannot rival what lives there. I am not more beautiful than what sea nymphs dwell at its surface. I am not even as beautiful as the shiny, scaled fish that jump and scatter. But I say that I am all that and more, in the tilt of my hip beneath this too-thin dress, in the lick of my tongue across my sun-peeled lips. They'll say I didn't understand the consequences, but oh, I do. I understand every one. And still I go forth. Still I put one hand out to touch the long curve of him inside his jeans.

He leans in and touches his lips to my mouth. It isn't a kiss. No. It's breath first. Just that. Then his lips harden, ask for something else; his tongue explores some inner reaches of me, something I couldn't know before. Another universe filled with teeth as hot and white as stars.

I suck his tongue into my mouth. Beneath the burnt tobacco and marshmallow, there it is: the young green. The taste of something unbreakable. I lean back against the tree-bark rivers, feel their banks shift and turn against my back.

"This won't go unpunished," he says. "You know that, don't you?"

I'd say yes again, but my mouth is tired of that word. I want to be silent now. I want to close my eyes and feel the hard future tightening around my waist. I don't want to think about her eyes watching or the man in my cabin or the blue dawn coming and the day that will arise from it. There is no hero in this myth.

His hands loop my wrists. The chain from pocket to wallet is longer than I expected. He slides it from the belt loops of his jeans. The cold heavy metal wraps my waist and the tree once, twice. I could breath if he wasn't at my mouth again, if he wasn't brushing one palm across the pucker of my nipple. He pushes my dress up, waist-high, chain-high, and the wind and his hands lick my thighs harder than the fire ever did.

His fingers reach in, sink into the place where underwear would have stopped them. I am slippery as the sea. More so. Not another boast, just truth.

He has two fingers inside me, his teeth twisting my nipple with that sear of pinch and pull. I struggle inside the chain. The tree bark scrapes my bared ass. I think it's running sap, but that's just me, wetting it beneath his fingers. He switches nipples, and the new pain is sharp enough to make me cry out.

"Shush," he says, without letting go of my nipple, sucking harder even.

When he has what must be four, five fingers inside me, nothing left for my clit at all, he drops to his haunches. His mouth finds the hem of my pushed-up dress, sucks it until the fabric is wet against my belly. He slides his mouth down farther, over the bottom of my belly, over the part of me that I shaved smooth, just in case, until he reaches the wet cleft where his fingers wait.

Somehow in the dark his tongue touches, scents, the center of me, touches the hot wet pulse in my center. I've had snakes there, all hiss and tongue, but they are no match for what he does for me. The tip of his tongue laps at me, sinking deeper and deeper until his stubble scratches the inside of my thighs. I buck against the chain around my waist, not sure if I'm moving toward him or away. I put my fingers on his head, deep in the soft, short hair, but he shakes my hands away. He is eating me alive.

This time, I don't cry out. I bite my lip to keep the voices inside. I wrap my hands backward around the tree, holding myself there as though the chain might break. If I were to come free now, I tell myself I would run, I would run back to the cabin and the man sleeping in the window light. I would go with the speed of light, with my winged sandals, and I would not be too late.

When he finally stands, I unbutton his jeans, pull them open until the zipper slides apart and they drop. He takes his own underwear down. He is the curve and strength of the Archer against my thigh. There are so many ways to tell this part of myth, but they've all been told before. Choose your objects: Bows and arrows. The slide of sword. The king's scepter. The queen's pride. This sea, taking him in. The serpent, devouring. If I could tell it differently, I would. Reverse roles, be the one who enters or the one who chains.

"Fuck, Cassie," he says, as he slides in all the way, pushing me hard against the bark, lifting me as high from the Earth as my chains will let me go.

I don't tell him he's confusing me with another girl. Wrong myth.

He takes my head in one hand, the snake and wind hair, and he pulls my mouth to his. Night wraps us in her helmet of invisibility, but not even that can stifle our voices. My sound is the crackle of the bonfire, the empty tongues of sky and wind. His is the hiss of paper catching light, the tumble of twig, almost breaking.

He fucks me, and kisses me with the tongue that tastes like me now, and for five seconds or five hours or five light-years, I am gone from this place, chained to my illusion of freedom. He gives me that, which is all I can ask. When he slides out of me, I slip down the trunk as far as the chains will let me. My feet touch back upon the Earth.

He lights a new cigarette—*click-click* of his lighter, hiss of smoke. He doesn't offer me one. I imagine he is watching me, but all I can see is the hissing flare of the red end. After a thousand hours, he flicks the end out into the dark air: Burning star, dying star. The final falling star of the night.

"I could let you free," he says. "Take you with me."

I want to say yes, but I know I've used up all my yeses. Try as I might to tell this story another way, it always ends with this.

He turns, and for a moment, I think I see the glint of silver sword at his side. A hero then, after all. But no, it is just his silver lighter. *Click-click,* as he opens and shuts it. And then he's gone, stepping back toward the campfire, toward that place where stars begin to die.

Somewhere, beyond my vision, a man in a cabin turns over in bed to find a promise has gone missing. The tree bark turns rivers to salt seas. There are no heroes in this story. Come the blue dawn of morning, I will still be here, waiting for my monsters. Bound by my own fate to the coming of the morn.

CARRYING A TORCH

Sophia Valenti

When Bobby comes in after his date, I pretend to be asleep. With my eyes shut tight, I listen carefully to all of the sounds he makes: the gentle clunk of shoes hitting the floor, the hiss of leather being drawn through belt loops, the rasp of his zipper being lowered, and the swish of denim being pushed to the floor. After a few more minutes of rustling, when he's divested himself completely of every last stitch of clothing, he slips between the sheets to take his place at my side. He's deliciously naked, save for what I've been longing for all night.

You see, I pretend to be asleep because if he notices that I'm awake, he'll insist on taking a shower before he comes to bed, and that would ruin everything.

Bobby and I have had an open relationship for a number of years. Our agreement was that we were both free to take other lovers, but aside from sharing names and general comments, we wouldn't discuss the intimate details of our affairs or play in the same space. He was worried that I'd be jealous if I ever saw him with another woman. And in one respect, he's right. But I'm not jealous of her—I'm jealous of him.

What I've been longing for all night is to breathe in the subtle scent of Sasha's perfume, her signature fragrance having anointed his skin as she writhed against him and marked him like the wild animal she is. It's not something that can be bought in a bottle, although once when I passed through Sephora, I recognized familiar floral undertones and my pussy began to instantly moisten. I lingered in the aisle, breathing deeply and squeezing my thighs together until a fellow shopper spoilt my fantasy by spritzing a spicy cologne. But that perfume had only been a hint, a tease. Because it's that delicious scent laced with the unique signature of sex that creates the heady bouquet inspiring my lust.

One night, I arrived home early from what was supposed to be a late-night date of my own. As I opened the front door of our apartment, I heard the sweet moans of a woman coming from our bedroom. After slipping off my stiletto heels, I crept across the carpeted living room, barely daring to breathe. The door was open a crack, and I peered inside to see a candlelit Sasha thrashing wildly atop my boyfriend. She was gilded in golden light that made her bare skin glow like that of an otherworldly creature. Her hips ground down against his pelvis as she took her pleasure from him, and she tossed her mane of dark brown hair behind her and cried out in ecstasy.

I didn't want to be her; I wanted to be her lover. How I wished I had a hard cock of my own, so I could feel the hot, wet velvet of her cunt envelop my shaft, her smooth muscles clutching my erection as she rode me to the finish line. As she came, her pussy would be irresistible, and I'd have no choice but to shoot deep inside her. Unfortunately, I had no dick to speak of, aside from the slim red vibrator in my bedside table, but I did have a pussy that was desperately aroused from the sight of this sex goddess in my bed. It was as if I were glued to my spot on the floor. I didn't even want to flinch, for fear I would cause this erotic mirage to disappear.

With greedy eyes, I watched Bobby lift her off his dick and toss her onto the mattress. I was pleased to see that she was shaved bare—nothing to hide my view of her glistening sex as she spread her thighs and impatiently bucked her hips upward. She was still panting from her orgasm as he covered her heaving breasts with kisses. My mouth watered as I watched him tongue her tiny nipples, first one, then the other, making them temptingly erect. I reached underneath my dress to slip a finger into my panties and stroke my dripping slit, wondering how those rubbery nubs would feel between my lips, how they would taste under my questing tongue. My pussy was sloppy wet, and as I fingered myself, I felt my juice drip down my palm. Bobby's lips traveled downward, peppering her nut brown skin with kisses as he grazed her flat stomach and her sleek mound. His head was blocking my view, but I knew the exact moment his tongue met her clit when she squealed. I pulled my fingers from my panties and sucked them between my lips, licking off every bit of juice as I pretended it was Sasha's honey on my tongue. My senses were suffused with the scent of pussy as she announced another orgasm, and I lapped at my soaked hand as I fantasized that it was my flicking tongue that had pushed her over the edge.

In a flash, Bobby was on top of her, fucking her fast and hard, which was my cue to leave. As hot as I was at that moment, I didn't want to get caught with my dress bunched up around my thighs and my hand in my panties. I quietly slipped out of the apartment and headed for the street. Outside our building, I propped myself up against a lamppost and lit a cigarette, taking a long, slow drag as I replayed in my head the hottest erotic scenario I'd ever witnessed. I was on my second cigarette when Sasha emerged from the building. Even under the harsh light of the streetlamp, she was gorgeous. I savored the sight of her full, red lips, sculpted cheekbones, and shining hazel eyes. Her hair was mussed in a completely sexy way and her face was still flushed. How many more times had she come while I lingered in the semidarkness of the street? My pussy throbbed relentlessly as I contemplated what I'd missed. I glanced down at my watch and saw that it was my expected time home. Bobby must've given her the bum's rush, not wanting us to meet in the hallway.

I didn't speak to her. I simply watched as she glided to the curb and extended an elegant hand upward, only to have a taxi immediately pull up in front of her. She flashed the driver an appreciative smile and gracefully slipped into the car, disappearing into the night.

With a sigh, I headed back up to our apartment. Bobby, already in the shower, called out a greeting to me when he heard my keys hit the dresser. I offered a hello as I stripped out of my clothes, noting the rumpled sheets. I climbed into bed, feeling the residual warmth of the recently parted lovers as I writhed in their love nest. I turned my head toward Bobby's pillow and for the first time detected Sasha's luscious scent. I rolled over and buried my face in the fragrant pillowcase, tilting my hips to hump the mattress and rub my swollen clit against the mussed bedclothes. I clutched the pillow, imagining that I was grinding myself against Sasha's supple flesh. Surrounded by the smell of her, I came in no time, stifling my cries with the fluffy sham.

By the time Bobby turned off the water and emerged from the steamy bathroom, I'd slipped into my robe and appeared to be working on a crossword puzzle, although in reality my mind was still preoccupied with images of the naked Sasha. He asked me if I'd had a good night, and I peered at him over my glasses as I truthfully answered, "The best." I saw a momentary flash of envy spark in his eyes, but I simply smiled at him and returned my attention to the newspaper in my hand. He didn't ask me any more questions, having had his emotions already unexpectedly tweaked. It was the first time I'd ever seen him act that way.

Since then, Bobby has avoided asking about my dates entirely, perhaps having been surprised by the light he saw in my eyes that evening, even though he didn't know the true reason for my excitement. One of these days, I'll tell Bobby that I spend my nights out with other men longing to be in his place instead. I'd trade it all in a second to be the one to tease Sasha's pert breasts and lick her dripping pussy until she writhes and moans so prettily.

After we come home from our respective dates, he's often hot to fuck—but so am I. I think he's trying to prove to me that he's a better lover than any of my other boyfriends. And I suppose that judging from my reaction, he thinks he's successful in his quest, not realizing that I've been dreaming of him for hours. While he's been out and wondering what I'm doing, I'm wondering what path his lips have taken and where his fingers have teased and pleased her—and where and how they eventually fucked. As I wait for him to return home, I mull over the possibilities and picture myself in his stead, my name on her lips rather than his.

So its nights like this I wait for, when Bobby comes home from seeing Sasha and slips into bed, thinking I'm already asleep. With the skills I honed during all of those method acting classes I took as an undergrad, I pretend to be in a deep sleep, but then I stir when he's on the edge of a dream and I feel him shift his weight on the mattress. It's that blissful moment when he's nearly lost in that twilit world that I snuggle closer to him and tease his neck with well-placed laps of my tongue. He groans through his sleepiness and turns toward me. I take his half-hard shaft in my hand and stroke it slowly, kissing his chest as I feel him swell in my hand. Before he's awake enough to protest, I slide downward and take his cock between my lips, sucking slowly and savoring the hint of Sasha's pussy that's been left behind. I take his cock down to the root as he tangles his fingers in my hair, encouraging me to deep-throat him. I know I can make him come in a minute, but that's not what I want.

I slowly pull my mouth off his dick, hearing him moan as the cool air hits his shiny-wet shaft. Desperate to feel him inside me, I urge him onto his back, then throw one leg over his hips and straddle him, my cunt hovering temptingly close. I reach down and grasp his cock, guiding it between my slick pussy lips. I've been wet for hours, waiting for him to return home redolent with Sasha's scent. I bury my face in his neck, breathing deeply as I grind my hips against him. It's those little hints of her and the knowledge that I'm going to ride him the same way she did that edges me closer to orgasm. Bobby thrusts upward to meet my crashing hips, and I feel a spark of pleasure deep inside that begins to smolder and spread. It's a delicious fire that is stoked by my cherished memories of Sasha and the laundry list of all of the dirty things I'd do to her, if only given the chance. I pivot my hips, seeking more contact with Bobby's body. I sit up and continue to grind against him, mimicking Sasha's passionate earlier dance and feeling my orgasm crash over me like a tidal wave. Bobby groans when he feels my cunt clutch his shaft, and I keep riding him until I feel the warmth of his come bathe my insides. Breathless and satisfied, we part and soon surrender to sleep.

One of these days, when the hunger becomes too much, I might confess my longings, but somehow I don't think he'd share—he's the jealous type.

OUT OF THE FRYING PAN

P. S. Haven

Lynn told me you came in her mouth," Lawrence began.

It's not like I expected small talk. Or even civil talk. We both knew why we were here.

But still I was caught off guard by his bluntness and had no response.

"Is that right?" he asked. "Did you come in my wife's mouth, Martin?"

I said nothing.

"Martin, listen." Lawrence moved closer. "I need you to be honest with me. Because I'm being honest with you. I promised you I would only do with your wife what you did with mine. And if you came in my wife's mouth I need to know so I can come in your wife's mouth. Are we clear?"

I nodded.

"And more importantly for you, I need to know if you didn't come in my wife's mouth. Understand?"

"Yes."

"Good. Now, did you come in Lynn's mouth, Martin?"

"Yes."

"Did she swallow it?"

"Yes."

Lawrence and I sipped our brandy in unison.

I glanced at Janet. She was sitting on the sofa next to Lynn. They were turned slightly away from one another, legs crossed identically, mirror images, as if each meant to block the other from her peripheral view, making it just a little easier to pretend the other wasn't there.

"Did you fuck her, Martin?"

"No."

"Don't lie."

"I'm not."

"You didn't fuck my wife, Martin?"

"No."

"Look me in the eye and tell me that."

I fixed his gaze with mine. "I didn't fuck your wife." I wanted to look to Lynn for support. *Tell him,* I was thinking. Tell him we didn't fuck. Then I looked at Janet, as if to reiterate what I had sworn to her a hundred times since last night. And I said out loud to her: "I didn't fuck her." But Janet wouldn't look at me.

Lawrence seemed satisfied. "What else?"

"What do you mean?"

"What else did you do besides come in my wife's mouth?"

"That's it."

"That's it? You did absolutely nothing else?"

"That's right."

"Did you not touch her?"

"No."

"Not at all? You mean to tell me that while your cock was in her mouth you didn't lay a finger on her, Martin? You mean—"

"Okay, yes. I touched her. Of course I did. I thought you meant—"

"I thought we were clear, Martin."

"We are." I looked at Janet. She was watching me now.

"Okay, let's try this again: What else did you do?"

"I don't know, we—"

"Where were you when she sucked your cock?"

"In the bedroom," I said and gestured down the hall behind Lawrence.

"I know that. I meant physically, where were you in relation to her. Were you lying down, were you—"

"Standing. I was standing."

"And Lynn was...?"

"On her knees."

"On her knees," Lawrence repeats.

"Yes."

"And that's how it was from start to finish? You walked into my bedroom, my wife got on her knees and sucked your cock, and then you left?"

"Yes."

Lawrence thought about that for a minute, then said, "Was she naked?"

"Yes."

"Completely?"

"No."

"No?"

"I asked her to leave her high heels on."

"And you? Were you naked?"

"No."

"Where were your hands?"

I had to think about it. "In her hair, mainly."

Lawrence thought again. Then, "Did you kiss her?"

"No." It was the only lie I told.

"Anything else I need to know?"

I shook my head.

Lawrence looked at his wife. "Is that it? Everything he said?"

Lynn nodded her head but couldn't make eye contact.

Lawrence stood and extended his hand toward my wife. "Okay, then. Janet?"

Janet stood and awaited Lawrence's instructions.

"Take your dress off, dear."

Without a word, Janet slipped the dress off her shoulders and let it cascade down her long legs until it formed a puddle of satin around her ankles. She wasn't wearing a bra, and the way Lawrence was looking at her breasts made me sick. It was the same way I had looked at Lynn's. Janet took her panties down and stepped out of them and the dress at the same time. She went to kick off her heels.

"No," Lawrence said. "You leave those on."

And with that, Lawrence turned and walked down the hallway and into the bedroom. Janet followed, completely nude save for her shoes. Once she had disappeared inside, the door closed and clicked quietly.

And the wait began.

After only a few minutes, Lynn stood and left the room. I think a part of me, a foolish part, had hoped that Lynn and I would do it again, that Lynn would suck my cock again while my wife did the same to her husband. But another part of me was glad she had gone.

The minutes began to accumulate. My mind raced. What if he was making her do more? I thought. What if she was doing other things? What if he lied to me? And then the absurdity of that thought hit me. What if I can't trust him? My cock was in his wife's mouth, my semen in her stomach, not twenty-four hours ago. And I was worried about me trusting him?

I tried not to listen for them, listen for their sounds. Then, just as purposefully, I would try to. I tried to hear Janet's breathing, her moans, the wet noises of her mouth. But I heard nothing. Not a sound.

Five more minutes passed. Then ten.

It was exactly seventeen minutes and thirty-seven seconds before the door opened again. Janet looked exactly as she did before she went it. I wasn't sure what I expected. I guess I thought she'd reappear and look the way Lynn had looked the previous night afterward: Swollen lips. Chin red from abrasion. Smeared lipstick. Mascara running in tributaries of black water-color down her cheeks. But no, she looked exactly the same. Even her hair was still perfect. She simply walked back in, got dressed, collected her purse, and asked me if I was ready to go. As if I would not be. No, please let's stay. Suck his cock again. Right.

Lawrence emerged from the bedroom, very slightly smiling, I thought. He, too, offered no outward signs of what had just transpired between him and my wife. And for a moment I allowed myself the pleasantness of hoping that maybe nothing had happened. There were no sounds, after all. No moans, no grunts, no agonized pleas of affirmation. For all I knew, Janet and Lawrence had simply disappeared into his bedroom, sat on the edge of his bed, and discussed how deeply hurtful what Lynn and I had done was to them. Talked about how this whole silly mock trial and punishment should teach us both an equally hurtful lesson. Decided that seventeen minutes and thirty-seven seconds was long enough to convince us that Janet had sucked Lawrence's cock to fruition.

But the look in Lawrence's eyes convinced me otherwise. And

the fact that Janet wouldn't allow me to look into hers. It had happened. They had done it. I was sure of it. And if I had any lingering doubt, it was dispelled when Lawrence said to me as I walked out of his house, "Now we're even."

THREE ON
A MATCH

Jeremy Edwards

I was eighteen, and I kept falling in love with my buddies' girl-friends. Bad habit, but I guess it was some sort of phase I was going through. They say that everyone needs a hobby.

As a kid, I hadn't been the type who automatically wanted what someone else had. But now, as a fledgling adult, maybe the real problem was that I was lacking in—well, confidence, of course—but also imagination. You don't have to use your imagi-nation to envision someone as a girlfriend, if she's already the girlfriend of somebody you know. The whole package is right in front of your eyes, day after day: a point of departure for the hard work your mind will be called upon to do late at night. Ready-made pencil sketches for when you turn your lights out in your room by yourself and start coloring in, supplying the details that you can oh so vividly conjure up, filling in blank after luscious blank. I wasn't lacking in imagination in that area, that was for sure.

The summer had been weird—riveting and mesmerizing, but

weird. I'd spent it playing third wheel all over town to my best friend Mitch and his honey Melissa, the cutie from Cutieland whose eyes glistened like Kool-Aid. When we were in Mitch's car, I felt like forgotten luggage in the backseat. When we were in my car, I'd sneak peeks at them in the rearview, and I'd see their hands going between each other's legs. It made me ache in a thrilling way, and I kept right on peeking, as traffic permitted.

One night I had to retrieve something from the back after I'd dropped them off, and I could smell Melissa on the seats. I don't mean Melissa's shampoo or Melissa's perfume—I mean Melissa. As far as my nose was concerned, her pussy was still my passenger, though her ass no longer warmed my vinyl. I closed myself into the backseat with her aroma for a while, touching my zipper reverently in the dusk—communing with an olfactory specter of the person I hungered for.

I'd been in love with her since about the second week in June. The high point of each day was seeing what pair of little shorts and which chest-hugging top she'd wiggled into that morning. (That is, I liked to *think* that she wiggled as she dressed.) As the three of us took big, greedy bites out of the hometown every night, in preparation for leaving it behind, I always tried to think of funny things to say—hoping to make Melissa laugh, to make those liquid eyes shimmer at me. When she laughed, I felt like I could see an echo of her cunt, ripe and juicy and receptive, rippling in her eyes. If I couldn't reach out physically and tickle her fragrant flesh like I longed to, at least I could tickle her mind from time to time and watch the nectar swirl around her irises.

As August arrived at its inevitable conclusion, I knew it was healthy that I was being forced out of the desire-steeped rut I was in. And yet part of me clung to an insane wish that this summer would never end.

* * *

College was a big new world, richly populated with instant heroes—like Colin, whose room was across the hall from mine.

Colin knew everything about the music we worshipped. In our circle, that by itself was enough to make him a leader. And the fact was that he was not only more knowledgeable than we were about alternative rock bands, he was generally wiser, more experienced, and more in control of himself. We were all freshmen together, but Colin seemed to have shown up with some attributes that the rest of us could only hope to grow into.

My friends Ed and Robby never commented on Colin's easy attractiveness to women. Maybe they didn't notice. I certainly did. I didn't begrudge Colin the way poised, cerebral, beautiful girls constantly drifted toward him. I would have, too, had I been a gorgeous straight chick rather than an awkward straight guy. Colin was genuinely kind and gracious and, with his chiseled complexion, he was handsome beyond his years. In my eyes, he deserved whatever nice things he was getting from these impossibly sexy women—things I often thought about at night, after I'd seen one of them float into his room.

And when, in late October, one woman emerged from the flock as Colin's girlfriend, I was as happy for him as an envious, sexually unactualized young man could be. I was sincerely glad that Colin and the lovely, magical Renata were fucking every night while the rest of us were studying or cranking tunes or watching TV. Hey, I was glad *somebody* got to fuck a dream like Renata. You don't want to see an allure like hers go to waste.

I was not so much jealous of Colin as I was jealous of myself—of a self I wanted to be but wasn't. Or wasn't yet. And I just wished, after the dorm went quiet each night, that I could slip into an alternate universe—for a mere hour—in which I was the one fucking Renata.

Where Melissa had been button-nose cute, Renata had an eclectic, unforgettable beauty. Her teeth were slightly crooked, which for some reason made her look very smart—which, in fact, she was. Her jaw was strong, while her voice was ethereal. Her blonde hair fell in thick, confident lines almost all the way to her shoulders, where it formed flirtatious curls at the last minute.

And where Melissa's presence had made me want to tickle her between the legs, Renata's made me want to spread her naked on my bed and solemnly lick her from her toes to the base of her neck—with special attention to her warm, blonde pussy, of course, and a premeditated detour into her sacred asshole.

When Renata winked that night in November, I thought I was going to have to transfer to another school. Oh, I knew she probably didn't mean anything by it. I happened to be walking up the hall, after studying chem with Robby, when she returned to Colin's room from the bathroom. She had her toothbrush and toothpaste clutched daintily in one of her perfect-as-a-painting hands, and she smiled and winked at me as she passed through his door. Her long tartan skirt swished, and then she was gone.

I told myself it had been just a cute, friendly gesture to someone she knew was a buddy of Colin's. And yet, I couldn't help imbuing it with waves of significance that rocked my insides. I took Renata's wink to bed with me, and in my head, the wink said, *Yep, here I go, Doug, back to Colin's room to eagerly throw my gorgeous nude body into his arms and coax him to do everything to me, till I pass out from pure pleasure. G'night!*

I jerked off furiously, three or four times in a row, and even after that I couldn't sleep. I didn't see how I could ever function normally again, being under the same roof as that wink. At about five A.M., I realized I was in love with her—that the wink had brought something to a pinnacle, something that had been building for weeks.

I was honest to a fault, so I told Colin that I was in love with Renata—just like I'd wanted to tell Mitch about Melissa. Unlike Mitch, who had a bit of a sarcastic edge, Colin was the kind of guy you trusted so completely that it actually seemed possible to tell him anything. So I told him. I told him at lunch, in the middle of the week. I think even savvy old Colin wasn't quite sure what to do with this. He ate his lunch.

Afterward, I wondered if he would tell her. Did I dread that? Did I long for that? I decided that both were equally true. *I want you to know,* I informed her in my fevered mind.

Next time I saw her, she flashed me a tender half smile. So she knew, I assumed. I found the half smile and its implications paradoxically chilling and comforting—and sexually exhilarating. Another sleepless night ensued.

In my obsessive inner world, I speculated that it turned her on, maybe just a little, to know that I had the hots for her. And that thought, naturally, turned *me* on—a lot. It was a vicious, delicious circle. And I was just going to have to fucking transfer. Sure, Colin and Renata seemed to be cool with the situation—but I wasn't. I was a mess, feeling more alive than I ever had before, unable to sit still in my classes.

The stereo was on, and Colin and Renata were drinking gin and tonics on the oriental rug. Yes—Colin, who wasn't rich but knew where to go for deals, had an oriental rug in his freshman dorm room. And, of course, he had a breathtaking, elegant girlfriend on his oriental rug, sitting cross-legged in a short skirt, her panties practically kissing Colin's magic carpet as she rode it.

Standing in the doorway, I was like a kid who'd somehow

stumbled onto an adult existence he desperately craved but wasn't ready for.

"We've been talking about you," said Colin, in a tone my SAT-trained vocabulary immediately labeled as *avuncular*. I'd known something was afoot when he'd phoned my room, asking me to drop by for a minute. Colin didn't normally ask us to drop by. He knew we'd show up, seeking his wisdom and advice, sooner or later—always prepared to come back another time if his door was closed.

I instinctively closed the door behind myself now.

"Would you like to spend a little time with me, Doug?" Renata asked abruptly.

"Huh?" I said stupidly. "What do you mean?"

Colin exchanged knowing looks with her, then grinned at me. "We thought it might help you get the whole thing out of your system."

I knew my face was as red as the official school sweats. I felt pathetic. "What, you mean like we go to the movies or something?" I asked weakly.

"No, Doug," Renata said softly. "Not the movies." Her weight shifted as she spoke to me, and I saw an instantaneous flash of pink silk lightning under her mini.

I was trembling.

"Think about it," Colin said diplomatically, relieving me of the pressure to answer. "We'll see you tomorrow, all right? We have some...studying to do." He beamed at Renata, who took a sensuous sip of her drink, and I virtually crawled back to my room. I threw myself under the covers and imagined what it would be like to lift Renata's little skirt up and bury my face in her pink, pink panties.

* * *

It was going to be the hardest thing I'd ever done, turning down this mindfucking offer.

But I didn't want get-it-out-of-your-system sex thrown to me like a crumb. Maybe I was a starry-eyed eighteen-year-old romantic...but I believed that if you were going to have a one-night stand with someone, it should mean she was actually dying for you to fuck her ass off, if only for the one evening. I really couldn't envision it as something she'd do just to be a good sport—as much as I appreciated the gesture, as much as my throbbing cock wished I could talk myself into going along with it.

"Renata is naked in your room. I walked in to see if you wanted to get together on the econ homework. Next time I guess I'll knock."

The trouble with Ed was that he had such an impenetrable straight face, I never knew when he was stating fact and when he was indulging his mischievous sense of humor. Did we even *have* econ homework? I couldn't think clearly. Was it worth quizzing Ed? I decided it was easier to crack my door open and see for myself how many beautiful naked women were, or were not, in there.

Renata was naked in my room. She had stretched herself out atop the navy blue comforter I'd brought with me from home.

When she heard me close the door, she propped herself up on an elbow. "Doug?"

"Uh-huh."

"Come here."

I came there. I sat down on the edge of the bed, on the edge of paradise. Parallel with her thighs, just a few inches from...

"Is this what you want?"

Reality appeared to have lost its grip on my world. "Uh... yeah, something along these lines. But—"

"Think about it," she said, echoing Colin. "I need a little nap. We didn't get much sleep last night." She turned over on her tummy—concealing the blonde bush I'd only begun to admire, but putting her heavenly ass directly in my line of sight.

I sat there awhile. *I'm hanging out with Renata's bare ass,* I assured my disbelieving self—making it sound like a social occasion. It was surreal sitting there in the silence, beholding her rounded, female flesh, inhaling the personality of her skin and her cunt, and wondering what was or was not going to happen.

I rushed to absorb every detail of her articulate nakedness, in case it was the only chance I got. I tried to savor her as my eyes roved over the slim grace of her shoulders...the seductive convexity of her hips...the private frankness of the small mole on her right thigh, and the slight ruddiness at the swell of her asscheeks, where the elastic of her panties had been digging in while she sat in class. The "imperfections"—a pitifully wrong word, as nothing could have been more perfect to me than what I was seeing—made it convincingly real, despite the wondrous impossibility.

After ten minutes of listening to her breathing—a sound that would have soothed me, had it not brought me to shivering heights of arousal—I woke her up. "Renata, I can't—"

"Before you say anything, let me explain. I'm not here just to do you a favor."

I had never been so confused in my life.

"I'm here to do *me* a favor, too. If you'll let me."

I just stared at her.

"After you left yesterday, I made a confession to Colin. I told him I'd been getting off on the idea that you, um..." She averted her gaze. "That you sort of liked me."

I swallowed, tasting the understatement in the air...and

reeling with the testimony that my obsession had actually been getting this goddess off.

"You're kind of sexy, you know that?" she twinkled.

No, I did not know that. Holy fucking fuck.

"What did Colin say?" I heard myself ask.

"Colin's a pretty understanding guy." She smiled, shyly. "In fact, judging from subsequent events, I think my confession turned *him* on." She licked her lips, evidently relishing a memory.

I was still trying to take it all in. "Does he know you're here?"

"Yes," Renata said quietly.

"Does he know you're undressed?"

She shrugged. "He knows I was undressed when I left his room to come here." She looked at me earnestly, and with a hint of impatience that flattered me. "I love Colin, okay? But I thought maybe you and I could just..." She put her hand on my thigh.

And then I was doing what I'd dreamed of doing. I was licking the sole of her foot.

When I'd been absorbed in my masturbatory fantasies, I'd forgotten to dream about how a real-life Renata would react. How she'd coo and writhe, and say the word *yes* in her crystalline voice. How she'd purr while flattening herself out, face-down, on my bed, so that I could paint her thoroughly with my adoration.

When I licked her calves, she relaxed so tangibly that I could feel it with my tongue. And when I reached the cavities behind her knee joints, she moaned. I looked up and saw beads of sticky fluid clinging to her pussy lips, the response I was bringing forth.

I'd never licked anyone before, and I'd sure picked a good

person to start with. Even in my horniest dreams, I couldn't have imagined this softness, this sweetness.

By the time I was licking her inner thighs, she was wailing—quietly, discreetly screaming in muted pleasure, with her hand emerging from underneath to dance on her clit. I met her hand there, bathing all of it—pussy lips, clit, elegant fingers—till the lips opened so liberally that I felt positively beckoned. Then I licked and probed within, while her bleach-white derrière bobbed above me. She came and came.

After that, as I'd promised myself, I licked across and up and down those delicate asscheeks, till my tongue nestled gently at the porthole between them. I licked around the ring, and flicked the tip ever so lightly inside her there. She came for me again, thrashing her head against the pillow I'd grown up with.

My cock was raging now, and Renata was rolling over and spreading her legs wide. I undressed myself and she watched me, running her forefinger along her sexy teeth. When, in all my scrawny naked glory, I got close enough again for her to grab me, she pulled me right onto her. Before I knew what was happening, I was all the way in her groove and she was humping me from below, her creamy legs holding on to me for dear life while my hands cleaved her ass apart, fingers in the crack. I was gone, shooting everything I had for her in the grandest moment I'd ever known.

And then I just had to lick her some more, continuing where I'd left off. I licked her belly, slaloming all the way from one side of her torso to the other as I made my journey upward. I lingered on her plump little breasts, coating the soft orbs and then teasing the nipples. She came anew, in giddy breast ecstasy, and I held her under the arms and tickled her sensuously, to add a layer of froth to the orgasm.

At last, when her rapture had subsided, I moved on. She

whimpered peacefully, contentedly as I licked her shoulders and her neck.

"You need to know, Doug, that Colin's never done that to me. Mind you, I'm not complaining about all the ways Colin makes me come. But what you did—fucking new one on me."

I wondered if there was something precious between a virgin and a woman he had thought was out of reach, something that made licking her all over a special kind of communion. Something she couldn't get from a sophisticate like Colin, even if he were to do the very same thing to her.

I'd had nearly every inch of Renata, and I knew it was an experience I'd take anywhere I went, through the still-inconceivable decades of grown-up life. Fuck, I'd take it to the grave—where I couldn't help imagining myself jerking off, under the covers of an implausibly warm earth.

But I also knew I was done with the business of falling for other guys' girls.

I stayed at that school, in that dorm, until I got my degree three years later. And whenever I saw Renata in the hall, I winked at her.

ONE HUNDRED DEGREES IN THE SHADE

Teresa Noelle Roberts

You don't often see one hundred degrees in the hills of central New York. It hit that temperature twice in one week, otherwise hovering in the high nineties.

Our air conditioner died from the strain, and every store in the area was sold out. We'd resorted to cool showers, lots of iced tea, and dips in Seneca Lake, which felt like a tepid bathtub instead of its usual glacial chill.

Sleeping was difficult, sex—or anything but the lightest caress in passing—downright impossible. Matthew and I clung to our own sides of the bed, desperately trying not to touch lest we melt together into one sweat-sodden mass. We clung to the weather forecast as we dared not cling to each other, praying for relief.

Finally, at the end of a one-hundred-degree day so humid we practically needed scuba gear to breathe, they promised a cold front, complete with violent thunderstorms. Knowing we couldn't sleep anyway until the heat broke, Matthew and I settled on the porch to wait. I sat on the glider, he in a camp chair, both of us naked because the porch faced the lake, away from the road, and we were almost too uncomfortable to care if we shocked the neighbors.

Touching with nothing but our gaze in the hot dark, we talked about all the things we'd do to one another when the heat broke. How I'd kiss and lick every inch of his skin, but not his cock—not until he begged me, and only when I heard his voice crack with frustration would I take him deep into my throat, working him over with hands and tongue until he filled my mouth with his hot come. How he'd lie over me, pinning me to the bed with his weight as he slowly worked in and out of my pussy, fucking me until my skin was on fire with need, taking his time until I was as slick with sweat as I'd been any time during the heat wave, but now because of our shared heat. Then, he said, he'd roll us over and let me ride him slowly and luxuriously to our finish.

I could feel the storm long before we could see or hear anything, an electric tension building in the sultry dark like foreplay. Matthew's words and my own sent butterflies dancing on my clit, but what I felt went beyond sexual. Even the crickets and night birds seemed to hold their breath, waiting for lightning. I could feel energy buzzing on my skin.

The thunderstorms rolled in around two A.M. Within minutes, the temperature dropped from Africa hot to warm but bearable. Just as quickly, Matthew moved next to me on the glider. His hand rested on my thigh and for the first time in what seemed like years, I didn't want to peel it away.

Lightning strobed over and over, illuminating Matthew's face and body. A flash of hard muscle, a flash of hardening cock, and then it was gone again, a repeated tease. Thunder shook the roots of the house with each flash. No time intervened—the storm was right overhead. Rain whipped sideways onto the porch, slicking our skin, cooling us enough so we could heat from lust.

We inched closer. My nipples crinkled, and it wasn't from the sudden change in weather, unless that could also make my pussy throb.

Driven by wind, the storm moved on fast. The rain continued, and a lightning show played out on the far shore of the lake, but it was no longer overhead, threatening the ancient oak trees surrounding the house.

Matthew took my hand, exclaimed, "Come on!" We ran off the porch together, into the cleansing, cooling rain. I was shivering within seconds, so used to being overheated that a normal summer temperature and warm rain felt blessedly Arctic.

Matthew's arms closed around me. Rain slick, his skin still felt hot against mine, or maybe the heat was inside me. It had only been a week, but I'd missed his touch so much.

His tongue parted my lips to dance with mine. My breasts pressed against him, and lightning shot into my nipples where we touched. He slipped one hand between my legs, rubbing and teasing at my pussy, which was as slick and drenched as the grass. A flash of distant lightning lit the yard as I clenched, shuddered, thundered under his hand. I clung to him, but my knees buckled, and he sank with me to the grass. The heat had turned it prickly and strawlike, but I didn't care and neither did Matthew.

We'd talked about slow and teasing and patient.

Instead it was hard and violent and welcome as the storm.

I raised my legs, wrapped them around his hips. He poised over me for a second, and as another flash of lightning turned the night to day, he rubbed his cockhead over my clit, against the hungry lips of my sex. I begged for mercy, but it was drowned out by thunder rolling across the lake, by the sound of rain against our flesh, by the roar of our blood. I arched my hips, grabbed his butt with one hand, his cock with the other, and guided him home.

Matthew's hips grinding against me, and his cock pounding deep inside me, and the rain adding its cool caress, and the storm rumbling and flashing around us added up to more than the sum of their parts. Added up to a cleansing, cathartic fury like the storm that cleared the air as the weather transformed itself. Added up to an orgasm that hit me like a force of nature, as close as I've gotten to the clichéd "instant orgasm on penetration."

Was this what being struck by lightning felt like? I couldn't move in any deliberate way, yet I couldn't stop moving—couldn't stop convulsing around him, couldn't stop clawing at his ass, couldn't stop shouting something that was only slightly closer to English than the thunder's rumbling.

If lightning had gotten me, it must have clipped Matthew too, because he was pounding crazily into me, and his face, when I could see it in the lightning's strobe effect, almost looked contorted with rage. Then he reared up, his elbows locked, his cock as deep in me as it had ever been, and called my name to the heavens, and I think it must have been chain lightning that time because I went off again.

The rain continued as we wrapped around each other in the grass, and we welcomed it, welcomed the cool that let us cuddle, welcomed thunder echoing off the hills. We lay there until another wave of storms pushed through, and one lightning strike came perilously close to us, and we ran back laughing to the porch. Where we made love again, slow and sweet this time on the glider while thunder and lightning played around us.

BURNED

Michael Hemmingson

1

Jordin Navarro was aloof, sitting in front of her laptop, naked, trying to finish her first novel one hot day in the middle of July, the Los Angeles smog seeping into the apartment like a midnight intruder bent on ravaging and pillaging unsuspecting virgins.

She was twenty-eight and knew she had to publish (let alone finish) her first novel before she turned thirty...or else she'd never obtain that goal: to be a hot young writer full of promise and aplomb. She had two dozen assorted tattoos from her neck to her feet: on her arms, back, lower back, ass, hip, fingers, and toes. She also had long red hair.

Her novel was a romance of sorts, about a threesome. It was generally autobiographical, as most first novels tend to be. She didn't know what to title it, though. By writing an untitled novel of romantica, she was hoping to rediscover what she had lost....

2

In the first chapter of this novel, Jordin's heroine, Dominique Speer, is a twenty-four-year-old architectural student living in Santa Monica, California (Jordin herself lived in Burbank). Dominique is an average girl with a dark complexion and long black hair with tints of natural red. Dominique is depressed because the guy she's been with since she was eighteen, whose name is Brandon Albert, has become far more aloof than the author; he's distant and uninterested in sex or love or the future and she fears the end of the relationship is around the corner like a drunk driver speeding his way to vehicular manslaughter. The novel opens with Dominique sitting in her apartment late at night, watching a David Lynch movie and masturbating to memories of better times with Brandon, when he was a confident young artist and working hard at his paintings and drawings. She is unaware that she is being watched; there is a man standing by her window and peeking through a crack in the blinds. He can see her by the light of her TV, and he can see her hand wandering between her legs. He is touched by her self-touch and the expression on her face when she comes. He falls in love. He waits and watches. Dominique goes to sleep around midnight. He makes his way around the back of the apartment and finds the kitchen window open. He uses a pocketknife to cut through the screen. He crawls through the window; he's cautious and quiet and he has a history of breaking into people's homes—only to steal things, not to rape. He has no intention of raping Dominique—this is what he tells her when she wakes up.

Dominique opens her eyes at 12:25 A.M. and can smell the intruder; his body has the odor of stale sweat, cigarettes, and the street. She sees his silhouette standing near her bed. She sits up.

"Hush," he says.

She wants to scream. She wants to get up and run, but she is frozen.

He sits down next to her. He's as nervous as she is.

"I'm sorry," he says, "I have never done anything like this, but I saw you through the window and you looked like an angel, a beautiful angel, and I had to come in and touch you."

He touches her shoulder.

Her body is shaking; she feels like she might vomit.

"I won't hurt you," he tells her; "I won't do anything against your will. I just want to talk to you, to see you. I won't rape or kill you, if that's what you're thinking."

She asks, "Promise?"

"Yes," he says.

"Shake on it," she says.

He shakes her hand: his is twice the size of hers and she doesn't let go of it. She thinks that if she keeps his hand with hers, he can't use it to hurt her. She doesn't believe his promise; she doesn't even know his name.

Nothing bad happens. He lies on the bed with her, holding her hand, and they talk. He does most of the talking. He tells her how he and his girlfriend drove out from South Carolina to L.A. in search of fame and fortune in the music business. He's a keyboard player and the girlfriend is a singer, but she left him for another man, a man with money, two weeks after the move. He's been in L.A. for a year, playing a few gigs, not making much cash, living in his car right now.

She tells him about Brandon. She doesn't tell him there are problems. She says: "I've been with him for six years and I love him very much."

"Where is he now?"

"Out of town. He's usually here."

"I'm jealous," the intruder says, "He has you and I don't."

He moves to kiss her. He kisses her on the forehead.

It is six A.M. The sun is starting to come up.

"I should go now," he says. He gets up and hands her a five dollar bill—"For the window screen," he says.

"Thank you," she says. "You didn't tell me your name."

"My name is Life," he says.

3

Jordin worked three or four shifts a week at the Happy Room, a topless dance club in West Hollywood. A shift was four to six hours; on a good night, she could make three- to four-hundred-dollars in tips and lap dances—on a slow night, one-fifty to two-hundred. It was an easy job—better than working in an office or retail.

She thought about her character, Dominique, and how Dominique was slowly losing her emotional core after the incident with Life. In the second chapter, Dominique tells Brandon about it. Brandon's response is: "I don't believe you."

Dominique is not Jordin, if that's what you are guessing; that part of the novel is not autobiographical. It is based on a real incident that happened to one of the dancers at the Happy Room, whose stage name is Mecca.

Jordin's stage name is Lira, by the way.

4

Mecca (real name Shannon O'Hannon) was twenty-nine and had been working as a dancer since she was nineteen, from Phoenix to Seattle to Portland to San Diego and now L.A. She was writing a screenplay about her experiences.

One day, a writer named Michael was in the Happy Room and paid for a few lap dances from Mecca. She asked him what line of work he was in. He told her he was a staff writer for a hit

TV show, and had written and directed a couple of independent features that were ignored.

"Really," said Mecca, "I'm writing a screenplay!"

Mecca wanted to pick his brain for information about the business; she managed to talk him into inviting her to dinner. After steak and a baked potato and a few drinks, she gave him a sloppy blow job. Three months later, they were seeing each other twice a week, so it was some kind of relationship.

5

There is a Michael in Jordin's novel, but everyone calls him Mike. Mike shows up in chapter three. He's a longtime friend of Brandon's, and he is also a writer—a novelist and journalist, not a TV scribe. Dominique calls him one night, asking if he knows where Brandon is.

She asks: "Is he with another woman? Does he have someone else?"

Because she has no one to talk to and needs to talk about the man called Life, she tells Mike. He listens to her ethnography. She sounds sincere on the phone. Mike realizes she is a human being with deep fears and emotions. He likes this.

The next two weeks, they talk a lot on the phone, then meet for drinks. He asks if he can kiss her and she says okay. He tells her he wants to sleep with her, but she is afraid, because there is still Brandon....

6

Mecca wasn't working the night Jordin stepped away from her novel and went to do a shift at the Happy Room—but she *was* there at the club, with Michael, and they had a bottle of very expensive tequila that Michael claimed he stole from some high-powered TV exec's party.

"I deserve this bottle," Michael said, "for all the changes he's made in my scripts, turning gold into shit, which in the end makes good television...."

7

At this point you may be wondering if either Michael or Mike are really me, your humble narrator, or perhaps both are based, in part or whole, on yours truly. Consider this: Michael is a fictional character in an unpublished novel and Mike is a real person in Los Angeles. I'll leave the rest to your imagination.

8

In chapter four, Brandon starts to realize something is going on between his old friend and his estranged girlfriend. One night, Brandon tells Mike to feel free to fuck his girlfriend. "She needs it," he says.

"You're serious," Mike says.

"She seems to be happier lately, because she has you to talk to."

"You don't love her anymore?" Mike asks.

"I still love her, just don't want to be intimate with her," Brandon says. "I'll tell you something," Brandon says, "for the past two years, whenever we have sex, I don't come. I can't come. I come when I jack off. I just can't with her. Why?"

"You know what would be good?" Mike says. "We should have a threesome...."

9

Mecca and Michael shared the tequila with Jordin. It was the best tequila she'd ever had—it was so smooth; it went down like water and didn't burn. Jordin wasn't a drinker, and she quickly found herself inebriated, snookered, smashed, shit-faced, three sheets to the wind. She was so drunk she couldn't dance on the stage. She started to cry in front of the customers. The other dancers and management were not happy in the Happy Room. The doorman/bouncer grabbed Michael by the collar and said: "I should break your fingers for doing that to her!"

"Hey!" Mecca said, slapping the bouncer on the head. "He didn't do anything, it's not his fault, she's an adult, she knows what she's doing!"

Jordin was sitting on the floor, bawling her eyes out, mumbling how hard things were, how she felt nothing, how she was going nowhere, how she was afraid of failing if she didn't publish her first novel before age thirty.

"She's your responsibility then," said the bouncer. "Get her out of here. And don't let her drive."

"Let's take her back to your place," Mecca told Michael; he lived two blocks away from the stripper club.

10

In chapter six, Dominique is agreeable to a threesome. The idea turns her on more than she wants to admit—the *idea*, in theory, that is, because she isn't sure if she can actually go through with it when the time comes.

She wants this to happen in neutral territory and suggests a motel room. She thinks going out of town would be good.

So in chapter seven, the three of them drive out to Palm Springs to do the deed. It is an hour and a half journey from L.A. to the desert getaway. It is awkward. There is tension. There is uncertainty. Brandon is uncomfortable. They talk about trivial things, not about sex or what is going to happen.

Chapter eight: they have arrived in Palm Springs and check into a motel. More and more, it seems that Brandon is not keen on the whole thing.

"I'll go get some booze," Brandon says.

Brandon leaves. He's gone for a while. Mike and Dominique sit on the bed and start kissing. He reaches under her skirt and touches her; she has thick pubic hair, which is different because women usually shave most, if not all, of it off these days; he inserts two fingers inside her pussy, which is very, very wet. "You make me so juicy," she says. "I've never been this way before."

She comes twice. The second time she squirts.

"That's the best hand job I've ever had," she says.

Brandon returns, catches them kissing. He stops and stares and looks hurt. He can smell her pussy in the air and knows something happened while he was out.

Brandon has bought a fifth of vodka, a half-gallon of milk, and a bottle of Kahlua. There are no cups, though.

"I'll get cups," Brandon says, and leaves quickly.

"He's backing out," Dominique says.

"He'll be okay," Mike says, "he wanted to do this."

"*I* want to do this," she says, and they start to kiss again....

11

At Michael's apartment, Jordin stopped crying and wanted more tequila. Jordin grabbed Mecca and kissed her. This wasn't the first time these two had been close. Lesbian encounters among the dancers at the Happy Room, or any stripper club, were commonplace. "Kick back and watch the show," Jordin told Michael. He did. He witnessed the two girls undressing, getting on his bed, making out, and going down on each other. Then he joined them....

12

For chapter nine, Jordin decides to turn up the heat, the romance, the depravity. *It's time to pork*, she thinks as she types away on her laptop. The three are on the bed. Mike starts to undress Dominique. She's shy at first, but gives in. She keeps looking at Brandon, urging him to be aggressive. "Come here and rip my bra off," she says. Mike agrees. "Tear her panties off," Mike says. Brandon is rubbing one of Dominique's legs, but he can't move. He can only stare. He doesn't believe he is here, that he agreed to this, that he is going to allow his longtime buddy to hump his long-term girlfriend.

"I've read Paul Bowles and Henry Miller," he says softly; "I'm hip."

"What's wrong?" Dominique inquires, her voice soft with the pain of six thousand years of hurt women.

"This is what we came here for," Mike says, annoyed.

Brandon stands up. He says: "You two go for it. I'll watch."

"What?" Dominique says.

Mike says: "Why don't you draw us?"

"Good idea," Brandon says. He gets his sketchpad and sits on the floor and says: "Go ahead and do what you want, I'll draw."

"Fuck it," says Dominique, "fuck him," she says and looking at Brandon she adds: "Fuck you, you coward, you Nancy boy, you impotent fuck, I'm going to suck cock and take it in my asshole like you've never seen porn before."

"Hey hey," Mike says.

"Just *fuck* me," she says, "and make it good...."

13

Mecca woke up first, in bed with Michael and Jordin—who were both cuddling and spooning and lightly snoring. Mecca didn't care for that sight. She got out of bed, put her clothes on, and left. Before departing, she stopped and turned to the two sleeping bodies and muttered, "I hate you people...."

14

Chapter ten has Brandon trying to draw. He can't do it. All he can do is look at the floor. He peeks up now and then, but it's too much—to see them kiss; to see Mike stick fingers in Dominique's ass; to observe them do the sixty-nine position while she faces Brandon, stares at him the whole time. He begins to weep; he didn't realize he had so many powerful emotions inside him, wanting out....

15

Jordin woke up and freaked. She had no idea where she was or how she got there. She was in bed with a man she didn't know and could only assume the worst. Michael woke up and said: "Hey."

She punched him in the face and jumped out of the bed, naked. She looked around for her purse, found it, grabbed it, and took out the switchblade she always kept for protection.

16

In chapter eleven, the drive back to L.A. is very uncomfortable. Brandon refuses to talk to either Mike or Dominique. They drop him off where he works and he walks away, not saying good-bye. He is disgusted, but not with them—with himself. Mike and Dominique go back to her place and cuddle in her bed. Chapter twelve: lots of sex scenes, with some romance.

Chapter thirteen: Dominique tells Mike she loves him. He says it is too soon.

Chapter fourteen: Brandon tells Mike he is okay with everything, even though he is not. He keeps his jealousy buried deep.

Chapter fifteen: Mike has a one-night stand with an eighteen-year-old hottie. He tells Dominique about it and she gets very upset. He goes: "We're not in a committed relationship, you can go out and screw any guy you want and it wouldn't bug me."

Chapter sixteen: Dominique shows up at Mike's home, drunk. She is holding a bottle of cheap, foul tequila. She demands to know why Mike does not love her. Mike says he could love her, but it's too soon. Dominique strips all her clothes off and says: "Is this body good enough for you?" Mike reaches out to her and says: "I will make love to you." She throws the tequila bottle down, smashes it on the floor, falls down, and starts to roll over the glass, cutting herself. She crawls to him, bleeding. "*This* is my passion," she says.

17

Jordin tried to stab Michael with her blade. She chased him around his apartment, screaming that she would get even for his taking advantage of her.

Michael pleaded for her to stop, not hurt him, not cut him, not stab him. He said, "Don't you remember last night, when Mecca and I came into the Happy Room?"

Jordin stopped, holding the knife in the air like a magic wand, like she was a character in a J. K. Rowling book.

She started to remember....

"Oh, no," she said, "I'm sorry...."

She sat on the bed and sobbed, hands covering her face. He sat next to her and held her. She leaned into his chest and wept even more...she grabbed him hard and asked him to forgive her.

"I finally *feel* something," Jordin said: "It burns."

That's it! She had the title to her novel!

ONE HOT SLUT

N. T. Morley

Just getting it shaved is like an epic feat. If you've never tried to shave one, I don't think you can even conceive of just how many nooks and crannies they have. If you have tried to shave a pussy, and you're not with me on the idea that this is a less-than-easy task, then you're way more coordinated than me, which probably wouldn't surprise anyone who knows me.

Once I get it shaved, though, it's pretty fucking awesome: smooth and slick and sensitive. After I finish I lean up against the wall of the shower and spread my legs and get the shower massage down there and rinse...and the warm water feels so fucking good on my pussy that I alternate between that and my fingers for about ten minutes, just kind of touching myself. Not wanking—well, not exactly, though it definitely starts to feel good. My clit feels moderately more sensitive, definitely, but FUCK!! It's really the rest of me that feels totally new and intense and incredible. When I touch my outer lips it's like they've never been touched before. I want your fucking tongue down there. I want you to fucking lick me till I go crazy. I want you to lick me till I come.

Which I might do any second, I realize, if I keep rubbing myself like this.

But that's just the beginning, really, because my shaved puss is not the first thing you're going to see when you get here. In fact, it might be quite a long while before you *do* see it, up close and personal at least, because I've already decided that as soon as you're in the door I'm going to get your pants open and suck your cock, which is why the bright red lipstick sits on the sink half opened and glistening; I was experimenting earlier. It's a deep ruby red color, the kind a girl wears when she has absolutely no reason to wear it except to make her lips look good gliding up and down a cock, which is why I got kind of wet earlier and decided to shave my puss.

And it's shaved, and I like it. It's shaved smooth along with the rest of my body: my slim legs, my dainty pits, everything except the hair on my head—but that, too, is altered. I spent three hours in the salon earlier today. Gone is the straight dark librarian hair I've sported since high school; I'd already decided to cut it short, so I figured why not one last fling with it, and if peroxide fries it, *c'est la vie*. It didn't get fried; it actually turned out pretty good, the color of pale straw and with about three times the volume it had before. I stand nude in the bathroom and curl and spray and fluff and tease my new platinum blonde mane until it's the revenge of the '80s super-starlet. *Oh, my fucking god*, I think, as I look at myself in the mirror. Naked, without makeup, I already look like one hot slut, baby, a seriously hot fucking slut for you. I look like a whore, my hair cascading everywhere and just begging to be grabbed, grabbed hard, and pulled, and my face—*Okay, no more thinking about that,* I tell myself, taking a deep breath; if I get too worked up I'm never going to bother getting dressed, and when you get here you'll find me naked on the bed—which I'm sure would be fine, but not at all what I have planned.

What I have planned involves a mesh black garter belt and fishnet stockings. What I have planned involves me wearing a tight, tiny little see-through thong that I wriggle my snatch into and settle onto my hips with the string tugging deep in my ass...but not wearing it, understand, for very long. What I have planned involves six-inch fuck-me heels that I can barely walk on, a push-up bra that turns A-cups into B-cups—look! cleavage!—and a cheap little black choker I got at Beadland that if I play my cards right you'll get the message is supposed to look like a dog collar. What I want tonight is for you to rip off this tiny black dress, fucking *destroy* it with your hands if you want, baby, or just yank it up and use me.

What I have planned involves a great big mop of blonde hair in a teased-out fuck-me 'do that's about as classy as a truck stop blow job. What I want, tonight, is me black-eyed with eyeliner and thick-lashed with mascara, my lips pouty and bright red gliding up and down on your cock, my ass tucked high up into the air and just begging you to fuck it. You heard me. Listen to me very carefully, honey: you can put it anywhere. Because what I want doesn't just feature me with cocksucking lips, with a shaved pussy, with tits finally big enough, or kinda looking that way, for you to slide your cock between. I did intimate things with that shower massager, baby, things so intimate....

Tonight I'm your whore, bought and paid for, and you don't even need to leave a tip. Tonight I'm your tarted-up fucking bimbo, and I want you to use me.

I should say before you get here that none of this was my idea. It started...well, I don't want to go into too much detail, because

I'm honestly not mad or anything. Just kind of hurt.

It started one of those nights you worked extra-late. You know, one of the ones—it's hard to keep them separate, isn't it?—when you called me at nine to tell me you'd be home late. You've been doing that a lot, baby, and I think I've been a good sport about it. But this was a Thursday, baby, our four-year anniversary. I hope the mailman liked his new watch.

I called Jerri and Amy and they had just gotten back from a movie. They came over and we opened a bottle of wine—yes, that's where the Paso Robles merlot went. And the Sangiovese. And the last bottle of Two Buck Chuck.

I know you were saving that Sangiovese in particular, which is probably why I drank it.

I was kind of broken up about all the extra hours you've been working. I got majorly drunk and told them everything. By the end of it I was crying, baby, I was crying pretty hard. Don't hold it against Jerri and Amy that by the time we made it to the Chuck, they thought you were a pretty big asshole. But before the Chuck was gone, they'd hatched a plan to make you putty in my hands, and it involved an expensive bleach job and some delicate work with a disposable razor. Jerri's not as innocent as she looks. In fact, she was the one lobbying for the conclusion that you're screwing around on me. Amy said she doubted it, but maybe, and I was sure you're not. There's no way you could, baby, we've shared too much; you just couldn't do that to me. You just couldn't.

It's not just that you've been working late. It's that you haven't been that interested lately. I mean, it's been over a year since you started something. I know because I keep a diary. It's been forever since you grabbed me, forever and a day since you grabbed me and fucked me, forever and forever since you grabbed me by the hair, turned me around, bent me over and spanked me, and then fucked me silly. I can't even remember the last time you fucked me without being asked.

Don't get me wrong, baby, I'm not looking for attention, really. You know what I'm like; you've always known what I'm like. I don't need flowers; I don't need candy; I don't need soft romantic music and scented candles and the lights down low. I don't even need a kiss, baby. Half the time, I don't even want one. Any time you want, baby, you know—you have to know, I swear you have to know—that you're totally entitled to just grab me and do me. Don't wonder if I'm in the mood. Don't worry about making me come. Don't worry whether I'm turned on before you enter me. Don't worry about whether I'm enjoying myself. I'm telling you, don't even worry about whether you're hurting me. Hurt me, baby, fucking hurt me if it gets you going. And I'm not kidding, darling: You...can...put...it...anywhere.

One good thing about this house on Brennan Terrace, it's got a great bedroom. When we moved here from our loft downtown, on your insistence because we were going to start a family, I was reluctant because it isolated me from all my friends, from Amy and Jerri and all the others. But I liked the house because I liked the bedroom. I liked the sliding door onto the patio right from the boudoir; it felt dirty, luxurious, decadent. I thought it was a sexy bedroom; I couldn't wait to get a nice big four-poster bed in there and have you fuck me cross-eyed in it. I can't say you ever have done that, exactly...things got pretty lukewarm right about the time that we moved. But I'm still optimistic; this bedroom is going to see some action yet.

That's why I've gotten the bedroom all ready, turning it into our own little whorehouse/pleasure palace. Brand new sheets, eight-hundred thread count Egyptian cotton, bright red—scarlet like the letter that belongs on my puss. There are candles everywhere—a whole box of thirty votives, scented in musk and sandalwood, and thirty new holders. On the dresser sits a silken cloth under which rest four silicone cocks of steadily increasing size, the largest one big enough to make my eyes water just looking at it—I hope you'll put that somewhere interesting, baby; I get wet just thinking about it. There's a vibrator and a black-and-silver pair of nipple clamps, with a shiny silver chain. There's more lube on the nightstand and a box of rubber gloves and a half-dozen condoms sitting on top of a big wooden paddle in case you miss the way I'm planning to wiggle my butt against you asking for it. I've got porn playing on the twenty-four-inch bedroom TV—dirty stuff, a four-hour DVD of nasty hair-pulling anal threesomes and gangbangs, women being fucked and spanked and double-penetrated, come on their faces, come in their hair, come all over their tits. Dirty, filthy stuff, a DVD it made me kind of wet to buy in that disgusting little sleaze shop downtown by the train station. The volume's all the way down for now, but I'll be happy to turn it up when we get started. If you want, baby. If you'd like that. If that would turn you on.

I'm not playing music because soft music would be cheesy, not at all what I want—and loud, pumping, earth-pounding ass-whacking hardcore would drown out your words when you talk dirty to me as you're fucking me hard from behind. Which I very much want you to do, baby—every dirty fucking word you've ever called a girl, do it to me tonight, baby. Slut. Whore. Bitch. Yeah, baby, even that one. Say it while you fuck me. Because I deserve it, I guess, I deserve it because this isn't the first time.

No, don't get me wrong, it's the first time for a lot of this. It's the first time for the shaving, and the slutty hair, and the candles and all that. But it's not the first time I've dressed up like a slut. It's not the first time I've wanted a man to grab me and fuck me and call me names. It's not even the first time I've wanted it…there. It's not the first time I've told a man that he could put it anywhere.

I know, baby. I know I said I'd never done it. I hadn't. I hadn't done plenty of things before the affair happened. It was maybe three months ago. And I could claim it was a mistake—I could claim that if I'd done it just once. Maybe even if it had happened twice. But no… I fucked this guy seven times, baby, seven times and a couple of blow jobs in between. Plus the hand job at the office party and about ten instances of serious phone sex.

If you read my diary it'll give you every detail of what he did to me and—Oh. My. God. It was fucking amazing. You can read it if you want, baby, you can read in my diary about how good I got fucked. I'll let you. If you want. But I won't tell you who he is, even if you ask, even if you demand to know. I won't tell you, because you might go after him; you might want to hurt him or something, and I wouldn't want that. Actually, it would be kind of hot, but it wouldn't be fair. It's not his fault he fucked me so good. It's not him you should hate, baby, it's me. It's me you should want to hurt. It's me you should be calling a whore, even if I like it a little too much.

I can't say I'm proud of it, baby; I'm not proud of cheating on you. The guilt's been consuming me. But I didn't know what else to do. He was there, he was hot, and he wanted me. He wanted me bad enough to do things to me I'd never been able to ask for with you.

I think it was a good thing for us, baby; I think I learned about myself. I think it'll be a net positive, if you can forgive me. If we can get past it. In the long term.

That's why I'm dressing up for you. I feel like a slut, and I want to be a slut—for you. I'm going to give you everything you ever wanted, and I'll never cheat on you again. I promise, baby. From now on I'm *your* slut, your little slutty whore. I'll do anything, anywhere, any filthy thing your mind can dream up.

When I'm all tarted up like this I can't figure out where to sit. I finally perch on the kitchen stool, because if I sit on the couch the dress instantly climbs up my thighs until it is far from decent. I've got the windows open and the curtains closed, fans going so it's nice and chilly; my nipples should be hard, and besides if it gets even a little warm in here I'm going to start sweating before I'm supposed to. I'm seriously hoping our creepy land-lord Bill doesn't pull one of his midnight garbage-rummaging trips looking for recycling, because what he'll find is more empty disposable enema bottles than any midsized city has use for in a decade, and if he spots me dressed up like this he's going to have very little question who's the culprit.

It's six o'clock, time for you to be home. When you don't show I get nervous; I change my thong, which is wet and feels clammy, and I fix my makeup and work on my hair a little. At six-thirty I pour myself a glass of wine. At seven I pour another, telling myself there's no reason to be pissed. You've simply forgotten. You've simply forgotten what I said this morning: "Be home on time. I've got a surprise for you." You've forgotten, and that's far from a hanging offense. I kick off my high heels, pour another glass of wine, and try to relax.

I'm on glass number four when the phone rings; I pick it up already knowing.

"Hi, baby," you say quickly, almost blurting it. "I'm sorry, baby, I have to stay late again. Tom has this problem with the Madrid project...."

Do you even remember? Even now, do you remember that I said I had a surprise for you? Have you forgotten my words entirely, or do you just not care?

Either way, I'd forgive you, baby. I'd forgive you, because you work hard, you provide for me, you're a good husband. Either way, I'd let it slide…if it wasn't for the laugh.

It's off in the distance—a feminine giggle, and the first start of a sentence. Coming out of the bathroom, probably, showering clean after she fucked you silly. Coming out of the bathroom and giggling to you how she's going to fuck you silly all over again.

But don't get me wrong, baby, it's you who tips me off. Because it could be a female coworker, stuck late at the office, coming by your desk and giggling for any reason. Any reason at all.

But if that was the explanation, you wouldn't cover the phone and make a hissing sound. And I wouldn't hear, distantly, a cruel hot whisper that sounds like "Sorry."

"Baby? Are you mad?" You ask me the question with guilt in your voice. I answer with a casual laugh.

"No, baby, of course not. You've got to work. It's no problem." I take a deep breath, because I've got to fight back the tears, but by the time I let the breath out I'm not feeling like crying anymore.

I say it before I know I'm saying it: "I'm going to go ahead and go out, then," I tell you. Now that the words are out, I can't stop—I just talk. "Amy and Jerri are catching a movie. I don't think it's over until after midnight. Maybe I'll even crash at Jerri's place; is that okay with you, baby? It's just such a long drive back from downtown that late." My voice has gotten terrifyingly even, the hint of cruelty in it doubtless undetectable to anyone except me, the slut of Brennan Terrace. I can feel the energy humming in my body, the swirling sensations of wine, the empty ache in my pussy that begs to be filled, the clean tight feel in my ass that says tonight I'll do anything—*anything*—and come home soiled and savaged, and never light candles for you again.

You sound distracted, baby. "No problem," you say absently. You even make a little sighing noise, covering it and pretending it's a yawn. Is she sucking your dick, asshole? Is she fucking down on her knees with her lips working up and down on your cock, the way I was going to be? Probably.

"See you tomorrow, then," you say.

"Goodnight, baby," I tell you.

You hang up with a sharp intake of breath—yeah, she's sucking your cock, or doing something equally nasty to you. Something I would have done, if you'd bothered to come home on time one fucking night.

Unsteady and slightly drunk, I pad into the bedroom in my fishnet-stockinged feet. I go around the room blowing out candles. In the slanted light from the hallway, I retrieve the condoms and lube and put them in my purse. On second thought, I go back in and get the nipple clamps.

I leave everything else intact, just in case you were wondering. Not that you'll care, baby, not that you'll care. But then I'm not sure I care, either; I'm not the kind of girl who does care, anymore. I'm one hot slut, baby, I've made myself one hot slut for you, and you're not here to see it. I'm the slut of Brennan Terrace, baby—and you can fuck yourself.

TRIAL BY FIRE

Bella Dean

We need to choose. Do you see any viable options?" Dave turns his face to the crowded dance floor. Parson's isn't exactly a swingers' meat market, but the place has an undercurrent of interest. And you can usually tell who's on the prowl.

I scan the club and sip my drink. I don't want to do this, and yet I do. Underneath my resentment and my disgust beats the steady pulse of excitement. And that simply pisses me off. "I don't see anyone. Maybe we should—"

"Don't start with me, Glenna. Really. If you do this, I'll know how much you love me." His dark green eyes, so impossibly hard and bright like raw emeralds: I can see it in those eyes. The absolute decision. I will do this or I won't. I love him or I don't. This is how it always goes.

This wasn't the first time I swallowed my argument. How did this prove my love for him? Was it that I was willing to do it at all? Or was it that I would later suffer the fallout? His jealousy, his rage, his doubt. Like the witches who proved their innocence by drowning in the lake or dying at the stake, I would go forward with what my husband wanted. If I did it, I loved him. If I got burned, I loved him. Then it would be if I loved him, how could I do it? And then he would break me down only to build me up again. I would go from saint to whore to saint all in an evening. I would give him his rush and then weather his doubts. Again.

I am not an idiot. Buried beneath is my own pulsing want. My own needs. The urge to show him. The urge to hurt him and bend him and—maybe just a little—break him.

"I think him. He's looked at you about six times in five minutes." I can hear the excitement in Dave's voice. I can see the need all over his face. I can read it like a sign. He needs a fix.

I look where he points and smile. I can live with this. He is very tall and very lean. Muscles run up his arms and his back, but they are not overt. Subtly sinuous beneath his formfitting Henley; these are not showy muscles. He is built like a man who works lifting or bending or building. His hair is dark, shot with gray. And I'm willing to wager his eyes are a wonderful dark shade of brown. But they could be green or blue. The truth is, I simply don't care. I like what I see. I like it even more when he smiles at me and my pussy jumps with an intense rush of arousal. I am wet before I can return the smile.

Dave motions him over and the man comes, looking confused but friendly. They lean together, dark blond husband speaking to tall dark stranger. I shift on the bar stool so I have something to do. It's a mistake. The motion and the friction serve as a reminder of what I will do and what I want to do, triggering more wetness, more breathlessness, more staggering jumping beats of my heart. Finally, they both turn to me and smile. They both look eager.

I am disgusted. And I am thrilled. I am about to burn.

His name is Sean and he is married. For whatever reason, the married part makes it that much better for me. One more layer of perversion. One more level of deceit. He looks very much at home in our living room, sprawled graceful and average on our russet-colored sofa. "So, do you do this...a lot?"

Dave sits in the corner. He covers up the dark brown chair like a shadow. He is broad, my husband. He is big like a bear and when he is angry, he reminds me of one. He shakes his big head and says, "A few times a year. Tell her to get undressed."

Sean blinks uncertainly, turns to me, frowns a little. Then he gets himself under control and says, "Get undressed, Glenna. Please."

"Don't say please again," Dave says, and then all that can be heard is the rustle of my clothes as I peel them off.

When I'm there before him bare, my husband says, "Put your tongue on her. Tell her to spread her legs."

I wait for Sean to order me and I do what he asks. His tongue is foreign. Broader than my husband's. Wet and sweet and forbidden. I am entering the territory of whore, leaving saint behind. I broaden my stance and let him suck my clit until I grab his shoulders to keep from falling. I come in a rush of shame and redemption.

I hear Dave sigh. It is an elated and exhausted sound. A paradox. Like his wishes. He loves it and hates it. I crave it and am frightened by the craving. "Now fuck her."

That's it. No more instructions. I don't look at him, but I can feel him there in the corner, like a predator and victim. He sits and watches as this stranger pulls me down onto his lap. Sean eyes his zipper, bulged by his hard cock. I take the hint and pop the button, pull the zipper. All I can hear is the zipper's tearing hiss and my husband's low groan. Both sounds make my cunt wetter than it already was. A deep-seated neediness builds up until I feel like my throat will close. I go slow to make Dave happy and make him suffer. I'm never sure which it will be. Part of me hopes he is in agony, feeling needle pricks of pain every time I touch this other man.

Sean's pale freckled hand pulls at my thigh, nearly circles it. He settles me on his lap and I feel his hot skin pressed to my wet slit. His cock jerks a little from the friction and he leans in and sucks my nipple into his mouth. The pleasure is intense and sudden. My head lolls back, my hips arch forward, and all the way I can feel Dave's eyes on me. I push my ass out: I want him to watch me. I want to look like art, something to be cherished and loved. "Put me in you," this stranger says and I do.

I push the silken head of his cock to my pussy and lower myself like I have all the time in the world and no interest. My heart is beating hard and I'm lightheaded. I push back the urge to just sink down on him fast and start moving. I want to go slow. I want Dave to get his fill. And me mine. I have fully entered whore territory.

He is different, his cock is different. It fills me in an unfamiliar way. But his mouth is hot on my skin and his hands are eager. He surges up under me even as he yanks me down and my body betrays me. It will not wait for me to be ready to come, it will come when it's ready. My pussy grows tighter and tighter still, that all too familiar feeling that signals the beginning of the end. "That's it," Sean says, because he may be a stranger but he's not stupid. He leans in, bites my breast, and the echo of his small violence shudders through my cunt. "Come for me, Glenna. Won't you?"

He has just left me a souvenir. The skin stings and thuds with my heartbeat. Tomorrow it will be a purple bruise, as effective as a scarlet letter. It is right over my heart.

There is a lazy kind of satisfaction in his voice that makes me both like him and despise him. His thumb finds my clit, his hand trapped between us. He presses, circles, presses, and I come loudly—for my husband, for myself, and for this new person who I will hopefully never see again.

And then Sean gives in and he is coming too. Dave will not come just yet. Dave's orgasms are private.

There is a flurry of activity as my husband escorts my throw-away lover out the front door. But this one surprises me, because before he can be rushed out, Sean leans in and kisses me—chaste and nearly sweet, right on the lips. For a split second, I wonder what his cock would taste like on my lips and on my tongue. I shake the thought off and wave good-bye.

The words are out before he's over the threshold. "You whore."

I wait—still, silent.

The door bangs with his huge rage. His big red, welcomed rage. This is part of his release. "How could you do that? How could you let *him* do that? You fucking slut. You dirty filthy little bitch."

He's breaking things. There goes my wine glass and then a cheap vase. He throws my stockings in the fire and watches them incinerate.

I have learned this part well. I say nothing. No arguments or pleas. No apologies or defense. I put my head down and I wait.

"Glenna? How?"

Nothing. I press my lips together. My husband, strong and big by nature, is crumbled by the act he himself has asked me to perform. He drops to his knees, crawls to me, puts his head against my still naked body. He pushes his face to my pussy and I wait. I hold my breath and my ears ring. "How?" His voice is now a plea.

I put my hands in his hair, a clearly comforting gesture. I

stroke and soothe and wait. "How," he says again but he has turned his face to me and is licking with long even strokes over my twice-abused clit.

It steals my breath every time, this whole damn scenario. The dark secret part of me that loves it revels in the perversity. I spread my legs, let him in. When he's wrung two short, sweet orgasms from me I help him. He is unsteady and dazed, drunk on his own sick fantasy. I pull his slacks off and wait. It changes here: I'm on top, he's on top, standing, sitting. Sometimes in his rage and self-induced hurt he takes me from behind, pushing into my ass like he is punishing me.

Not tonight. Tonight it's sweet. Tonight he lays me back like a new bride and climbs between my parted thighs. His eyes shine, softer than back at the bar, unfocused and humbled. "It's okay. It's okay," he says, kissing along my neck. Now he is soothing me. He is reassuring me. "I know why you did it, Glenna."

Because you asked me to...

"I'll forgive you. I love you. And you love me. I know you do."

"I do." *Look what I do for you...*

The dark part of me laughs. Because it's also for me; I am simply loath to admit it.

"Glenna, Glenna, the good witch." He sighs his pet name for me as he fucks me. Harder and harder and we both spiral down into our sinister pleasure. And here is his private orgasm. His dirty little secret. Coming where another man, a stranger, has already come. But I don't like him to be alone in this thing so I come with him, a warm but shallow orgasm.

For now I am redeemed. For now I am good. I am back in the land of saint. Until my next trial by fire.

WHERE THERE'S SMOKE

Kristina Wright

Is his cock bigger than mine?"

Daniel is on top of her, inside her, when he whispers his urgent question. Megan's eyes fly open and she stares at him in the dim light of the bedside lamp. Daniel's words have pulled her away from a very dirty fantasy about Adrian Grenier and, consequently, away from her orgasm.

"What?" she gasps as he thrusts into her. "Who?"

Daniel stares at her, all dark-eyed intensity and possessive masculinity. "I know about him. You don't have to lie."

Oh, shit. That is her first panicked thought. Then, *How did he find out?*

She almost blurts out what she is thinking. Instead, she takes a breath and says, "What are you talking about, Daniel?"

She has been so careful. So very, very careful. She loves Daniel. They have been married for seven years, most of them happy with the exception of a rough patch here and there. Richard came along during one of those rough patches: a comforting shoulder to cry on, a friend to share coffee with; an older man who knew the ups and downs of marriage because he'd been married for nineteen years himself. She has no intention of divorcing Daniel. For that matter, she has no intention of ending her relationship with Richard, either.

"I just want to know if his cock is bigger than mine," Daniel says insistently. He pushes her knees back to her chest; she gasps as he slips deeper. "Does he fill you up?"

Megan has no idea what crazy game Daniel is playing. He doesn't seem angry to know she has a lover—quite the contrary. He is hard and thick inside her, sweat glistening on his brow. He wants her, that much is clear. But she doesn't know why he initiated this little late-night tryst before asking her about her extra-marital affair. She turns her head away from him, mind racing. Her body doesn't care about the battle her mind is waging, she is wet and hot and her pussy ripples around Daniel's cock.

"Mmm, I bet you're thinking about him right now. I can feel your pussy squeezing me."

She moans, feigning mindless arousal to buy herself some time. What should she say? Does he want her confession like this, while they're making love? What is he trying to prove? She feels a rush of conflicting emotions: guilt, remorse, anger.

Arousal.

He stretches over her, nuzzling her neck. "Just tell me, Megs. Tell me how big his cock is."

Why would a man want to know that? She can't begin to imagine why Daniel is obsessed with the size of Richard's cock, but she's not thinking of Adrian Grenier anymore. Now she is thinking about her lover's cock.

"It's huge," she blurts out.

It's not even true. Richard does have a nice, thick cock, maybe a couple of inches longer and a little thicker, but it isn't *huge*. She hadn't even really thought about comparing the two until Daniel asked. She envisions the two men side by side, cocks hard for her, and a moan escapes before she can stifle it.

"Huge, huh?" Daniel has gone still inside her.

Shit. She should have kept her mouth shut. He didn't really want to know. She closes her eyes, waiting to feel him pull away. Her fists are clenched in the sheets. Her orgasm has completely left the building. What in the hell was Daniel hoping to get from this?

Then he begins moving again, sliding out slowly until the head of his cock is barely nestled in her pussy before pushing back inside her. Again and again, he moves slowly inside her, teasing her. "Tell me," he growls. "Tell me about your big-dicked lover."

The whole thing is surreal. This is Daniel, for god's sake. Daniel, who got jealous when she told him the barista at the coffee shop had started giving her free coffee when his boss wasn't around. Daniel, who doesn't like to overhear her gossiping with her girlfriends about ex-boyfriends. But here he is, fucking her like a man possessed, not possessive, asking her about her lover.

Desire, hot and wet and needy, curls tight in her belly. Scared as she is, Daniel's words and intensity are driving her back toward orgasm. She wraps her legs around his back, pulling him into her.

"What do you want to know?" she whispers in his ear, digging her nails into the muscles of his shoulders. "What do you want to know about my lover?"

The words are naughty, delicious morsels on her tongue.

Daniel tucks his hands under her ass, pulling her up to meet his cock. "Tell me what it's like to fuck him," he says, his voice low and dirty, like an anonymous pervert on the phone. "Tell me how you fuck him in our bed."

She moans, clenching her pussy around him. How does he know? Why doesn't it bother him? She doesn't care anymore. Later, when they are done, they can have it out once and for all. But now, this moment with Daniel inside her, all she cares about is getting fucked.

"He comes over on Saturdays when you're golfing," she confesses. "Early. I call him as soon as you're out the door and he's here with the hour."

Daniel is still moving slowly inside her, listening to every word of her adulterous confession. "Can't wait to have him fuck you?"

She presses her lips to his neck and sucks hard. He moans, pressing his neck to her mouth. She thinks about sucking Richard's cock, how she can never get enough of him even after she's made him come. Does Daniel want to know that?

"I love your mouth, baby," Daniel whispers, and for a moment she is caught between the reality of being with her husband and the memory of her lover saying those very words just a few days earlier. "Tell me what you do with him."

She closes her eyes and thinks about last Saturday. "Everything," she says. "Anything he wants."

"Tell me."

A shiver dances across her skin as she remembers. "He tied me to the bed last Saturday," she says. "Spread open for him."

The memory is like a physical touch and she feels the goose bumps rising on her damp flesh: Richard tying her down, his strong hands running over her body, pinching her nipples hard until she arched off the bed and screamed for him to fuck her. He had fucked her with his fingers first, before pushing his cock inside her. She came so many times she lost count, straining at her binds until they left marks on her wrists and ankles. She won't let Daniel tie her up. She hates being out of control, feeling helpless and weak. But not with Richard. When Richard wants something, she gives it to him.

"Tied you up," Daniel repeats. "What did he do to you?"

"Fucked me."

"How?"

Should she tell him? Does he really want to know the details? There is enough of a survivor's instinct floating around in her fevered brain for her to think she should hold back the details. Isn't it enough that he knows she has a lover?

Daniel pulls out of her, leaving her suddenly empty, bereft. With one smooth motion, he flips her over onto her stomach like she is a rag doll; like he is Richard, taking control. With his arm under her waist, he raises her up on her hands and knees. A sharp smack to her ass makes her yelp, first pulling away, then pushing back toward him, wanting to feel that sting again, wanting him to warm her skin.

"Tell me how he fucks you," he demands again. "I won't fuck you until you do."

She whimpers. She's beyond caring what happens after they're done. She needs this. She needs Daniel. The realization is startling. She loves Daniel, yes, but she cannot remember the last time she *needed* him.

"He fucks me any way he wants," she says, feeling a warm blush spread through her cheeks. "He makes me beg."

"How did he fuck you Saturday?"

"Hard. Rough."

"Where?"

She flashes back to Saturday, the way Richard had fucked her, used her. The way she had begged for more even after she was so sore she knew she wouldn't be able to let Daniel touch her for days; begged for more even after Daniel called and said he was on his way home from the golf course.

"He straddled me and fucked my tits and came in my mouth," she says, remembering the way Richard had made her beg to suck him. "Then he fucked my pussy."

It's easier to say it when Daniel isn't looking in her eyes. The saying, "Confession is good for the soul" pops into her mind and she lets out a little hysterical laugh. She never thought she would be confessing anything like this: on her hands and knees, wiggling her ass for Daniel to fuck her.

"Dirty girl," Daniel says, giving her ass another smack. "Did you like it?"

She nods quickly, her long hair streaming down to cover her shameless face. "I loved it," she says. "I was so wet."

Daniel slides two fingers inside her. "Wet like you are now?"

"Wetter." She had soaked the sheets that day with Richard. She'd been changing the bedding to hide the incriminating evidence when Daniel came home. She wonders if he remembers. "Wetter than I've ever been."

Daniel pulls his fingers from her. "Roll over."

His voice is hard, demanding. She hardly recognizes it. Daniel is a sweet, gentle lover. But tonight he is someone else. Tonight he is more like Richard, which is why she moves quickly to obey him. Lying on her back, she watches him warily as he kneels between her open thighs.

"Show me how he tied you to the bed."

She shakes her head, her heart pounding. She doesn't know why the idea of letting Daniel tie her up scares her so much and letting Richard do it feels natural. "No, Daniel, I don't want to—"

"I'm not going to tie you up," he interrupts her. "You can save that for him. I just want to see how you were laying. Show me."

She slowly stretches her arms over her head, grasping the brass headboard. *This isn't so bad,* she decides, watching Daniel's gaze slide from her hands down to her breasts, then lower.

"And your legs?"

She spreads her legs wide, stretching them toward the corners of the bed. Though she's not tied, she feels helpless. She likes the way Daniel looks at her, the way his hungry gaze stares between her spread legs as if he has never seen her before. And perhaps he hasn't. Not like this. She feels out of control.

She finds her voice. "Fuck me," she whispers, her mouth as dry as her pussy is wet.

"How?" He smiles wickedly, but his eyes are dangerously serious. "Tell me."

"Hard. Please. Fuck me."

She watches as he takes his cock in his hand. She is arching her hips up to meet him, whimpering softly. He strokes the head of his cock over her sensitive, swollen clit and she nearly comes off the bed. Gripping the headboard, she strains upward toward his cock. She needs this, now. She needs him to fill her and fuck her and make her come. Her skin is on fire; she's panting raggedly as if she has run a mile. Richard does this to her, makes her feel like this. And now Daniel is doing it to her, too.

"Fuck me," she says, staring down her body at his cock barely brushing against her wet slit. Then she says it again, her voice rising to a pleading moan. "I need you to fuck me."

Daniel has the nerve to laugh. "You're so fucking wet," he says. "Are you thinking about him?"

She hesitates, meeting his gaze. Does he really want to know? She seems nothing but raw animal arousal in his expression. She nods.

"You like the way he fucks you hard?"

She nods again. "Yes," she whispers.

"Do you want me to fuck that way?"

She blinks, staring at him for a long moment. Does she?

"Yes. Fuck me, Richard." She didn't mean to say his name. She hears Daniel's sharp intake of breath. "I'm sorry," she says. "I'm so sorry."

Daniel is on her before she can finish her apology, his cock slamming into her, his hands wrapping around her wrists, pinning her to the bed. He leans over her, sucking each nipple hard, hard enough to make her whimper, hard enough so that she feels it in her clit.

"Say it again," he says fiercely, nipping at a tender nipple. "Tell him to fuck you."

She's trying to catch her breath, her body straining toward release. "Fuck me," she gasps. "Fuck me, Richard."

She grips the headboard as Richard—no, Daniel—fucks her hard, slamming into her again and again until the intense plea- sure makes her whimper. She feels full and swollen, her pussy gripping the length of his cock. Images, fantasies, flash through her mind: Daniel watching Richard fuck her, then the two of them taking her at the same time with Richard by the bed, offering his cock to be sucked while Daniel fucks her.

The combination of sensation and fantasy loosens the knot of desire in her belly until it finally, almost painfully, sends her over the edge into orgasm. It begins with a tightening ripple through her pussy, wet heat radiating throughout her as her body goes taut and still in preparation for the onslaught. Then she is coming with a scream, thrashing beneath Daniel as he fucks her faster, harder, making it hurt in that way she loves. Making her feel every inch as he fucks her, his hands digging into her ass, his head tucked into her shoulder as he whispers her fantasies.

"That's it, fuck him. Come on his big cock."

She hears herself as if from a distance, a wild thing whimpering and moaning, incoherent and mindless. All that matters is that she is coming, coming hard. It doesn't matter whose cock is slamming into her, coming inside her. She is getting what she has needed for so long.

He groans, arching over her as he comes, their bodies pressed together, his cock buried inside her. He is slick with sweat, panting in her ear, pressing her against the bed. She feels helpless, overpowered. Tears stream from the corners of her eyes, more wetness leaking from her body. Her physical release has triggered an emotional one and she feels raw, as if all the hard fucking has stripped away her protective barrier.

Daniel rolls off her, releasing her. She doesn't move. She still feels the aftershocks of her orgasm tightening her pussy, phantom sensations reminding her of what she just experienced.

"You can let go of the headboard," Daniel says, his voice rough with exertion.

She slowly releases her grip on the rails, feeling the blood return to her fingers. She lies still and quiet, afraid to say anything. Afraid of what happens now.

Daniel pulls her into his arms and cradles her head against his shoulder. She feels feverish and the close contact doesn't feel the way it did a moment ago, but she doesn't resist. She curls her hand on his chest, over his heart.

He kisses the top of her head. "That was incredible, babe."

She can't argue with that. It *was* incredible. The best sex they've ever had. Maybe the best sex she's ever had.

"Thanks for indulging me," he says, stroking her shoulder soothingly.

She is still afraid to move. She doesn't know the rules of this game he is playing. "Indulging you?" she asks, careful to keep her voice neutral.

"Yeah. I know it's not your thing, but sometimes it's fun to get a little kinky."

A thought flits through her mind. She is almost afraid to let it take hold. She pulls away, props herself up to look at him. He looks calm, relaxed; utterly satisfied.

"That was kinky?"

Daniel gives her an indulgent smile. "Well, kinky for you. Talking dirty about another man fucking you? You really got into my little fantasy."

"Fantasy," she says, almost in agreement. "Yeah. Where did that come from?"

He shrugs, looking bashful. "I don't know. Just a fantasy."

She nods. "Just a fantasy, huh?"

That familiar possessive look comes into his eyes. "Oh, yeah. *Just* a fantasy," he says, pulling her back down into his arms. "Don't go getting any ideas. I'm not sharing you with anyone."

"Too late," she breathes against his skin, too soft for him to hear.

A contented smile curls her lips as sleep tugs at her. She needs her rest. After all, tomorrow is Saturday.

TEXAS HOT

A. D. R. Forte

M ornin'," I tell him. "Better get that yard done before it gets too hot."

But it's already hot.

Texas July morning. Heat-soaked air, moist and sticky like my fingers on my clit as I watch him from my window: Shirtless, denim shorts. Skin glistening with sweat.

Can you work it, baby, like you work that mower? Those power tools in your tricked-out garage. Like you drive that big, badass pickup truck. Can you make my pussy cream like this and make me beg for more?

Someday I'm gonna find the nerve to ask him over...make him mow my lawn.

FLICK THAT BIC

J. D. Waters

Nine o'clock and I'm beat. Then she walks into the bar and the breath in my throat solidifies. I stop, right there, the glass halfway to my lips. She is small and compact, tightly wound from the looks of her. Her hair is pulled up and the color of spilled ink, black like sin. Her eyes are piercing, a deep chocolate that somehow radiates with an animal's sheen. She is perfect.

For the first time in a long while, my cock grows rigid in my pants. Not morning wood, or my wife putting her hand too high up on my thigh, but honest to god arousal. Watching her move in her deliberate lithe way, makes the urge to fuck her nearly unbearable. I glance around and am grateful that the only open stool is the one next to me.

She's behind a blonde woman. The blonde is about forty and wearing too much makeup and when she spots the stool and then me, her face lights up. I'm not wearing my wedding band. I rarely do these days.

The blonde reaches for it and I give her a regretful smile. "Sorry, I'm saving it for my friend." I say it with my eyes on the brunette who is now within earshot.

The blonde's smile fades and her cheeks color. I feel bad—but not too terribly bad when the petite creature behind her gives me a small mysterious smile and moves toward the stool.

The blonde storms off and I call out another insincere apology. I can feel the brunette sitting there, watching me—a shimmering hot energy that makes my cock twitch this way and that in my neatly pressed chinos. I loosen my tie even more so I can fucking breathe. My throat seems to be closing, and I can feel the fine pricking tickle of sweat coming up on my skin. "My name is John," I tell her.

She smiles a slow knowing smile and I can see her teeth, small and white and perfectly straight. I wonder what they will feel like marking my skin. She licks her lips, and I fight the urge to groan. Her tongue is petal pink and wet, the perfect soothing balm to the bites she will leave.

"Lucinda."

That's all. One word. Then she turns to the bartender and raises her finger. He's there in a blink. For someone so small, she has the presence of an Amazon, a way about her that commands attention and obedience. "What'll it be?" he asks, but he's staring at her tits, and I feel the urge to punch him in his flat, pockmarked forehead.

She puts her hand on my thigh and my anger evaporates in a heartbeat.

"Vodka, straight up, twist of lime. Make sure the lime's clean." She says it with a sense of ease, not one lick of worry that she might sound bossy or be inconveniencing an already busy man.

He smiles and it borders on a leer. Lucinda smiles back. The smile does not touch her eyes.

"You?" he nods his head at my glass that holds only a stain of whiskey at the bottom.

"He's done, thank you," she says and shoos him with her hand.

"I could have gone for another."

"Too much alcohol can hinder orgasm," she says and when her drink appears, she sips slowly. Each sip would not even fill a thimble.

Here she is exercising her first bit of power over me. It is all I can do not to touch myself through my pants.

When that seemingly endless drink is finally gone, she says, "What kind of car do you have?"

"An SUV. A Ford. Why?"

She frowns when I question her and says bluntly, "That will cost you."

A taut excitement surrounds me. My skin is wrapped in tight bands of anticipation.

We stand and I look down at her. I'm six-three. That's when some of them falter. The women I hope to bow down to. Oh, they talk a big game and then when we go to leave, there they are, looking up at me, and they cave. How can they dominate me? they think. If only they really understood how much I crave it. Need it. How I would obey them despite stature.

Sadly, most of them are not real. They cannot do for me what I need done.

"Well? What the fuck are you looking at?" she says and flicks a yellow lighter like she's dying to set something ablaze. "Don't make it worse for yourself."

She's genuine. She's the real deal.

She looks at me like she can read me, like she senses something in me. The real ones always do. I feel like I could cry with relief if I let myself. Instead, when she points to the door, I walk ahead and lead her to my car.

* * *

"Put them up there, John. Be a good boy."

She has yanked my headrest up to its tallest setting. I shiver in the chilly outside air. The car is not running and my shirt is off. I would give anything for a warm spill of heated air from the dashboard vents. Instead I grunt when she ducks her small head and bites my nipple. My cock jerks. My face floods with shame.

"Pay attention!"

I nod and try not to hump up at her. It's hard because she is straddling me, the warm seam of her cunt riding my hard-on through my khakis. She is tying my wrists to the metal struts that brace the headrest. The rope is from the roadside emergency kit. Finally, she yanks, and my bonds bite into my wrists, a rough painful presence. She wiggles some more as she reaches back and plucks a long, jeweled clip from her hair.

She holds it up. "Pretty, pretty, don't you think?"

I nod and try to swallow. The clip is about six inches long and made of silver. There are tiny jewels embedded in it and the small alligator teeth gleam dully in the glow from outside streetlamps. Lucinda had been pleased that my windows were not tinted. She told me that anyone could be walking through the parking lot and see us like this: me bound and shirtless, her straddling my lap with her skirt hiked up around her hips like a whore.

I arch up, just for one second. I press my cock against her heat and she says, "Bad, John. Now look what I have to do." She traces my nipple with the clip first, just to let me sweat. I want to beg her not to because that fucker is going to hurt. Any fool can see that. But I want to beg her to hurry, too. It's been way too long since I've had pleasure steeped in pain.

While she was runs more cold metal circles along my chest,

I have the chance to think. Think that I do not know her, that she could slit my throat while I sit here tethered. My cock grows more desperate and I hear my own eager breath. "Please."

"Please what? Please do? Please don't?" She trails the tapered tip of the clip down the center of my chest. It slides along my belly and I hump up at her again. "Uh-unh-uh," Lucinda chides.

I can only answer honestly, "Yes."

Then the clip bites me, cold metal jaws on the flat of my nipple. Pain shoots jaggedly along my skin, plucking my nerves. I dance a little in my seat and she leans in, licks my bottom lip, and then bites me there until sparks shoot off behind my closed eyes. I am panting. She wiggles in my lap like she's dancing.

"Please," I say again. I'm not sure what I mean, but I trust her to decipher. This stranger who speaks the same language I do. The language of pain.

She lets the clip hang there and the weight of it makes my pain heavy and dull. I feel my heartbeat in my cock and in my nipple that is being starved of blood. I try to breathe deeply, but I gasp instead. One tear gets free and with my hand bound, I am helpless to wipe it away.

Lucinda licks it off my face. "Nice. Salty. You'll be okay, baby. You're being a good boy."

I nod and she starts a slow steady rhythm on my lap. She is sliding back and forth, just an inch or two. Just enough to ride my hard-on with her hot wet cunt. She is pantyless and I can smell her pussy, smell her excitement in the now warm car.

I want to be in her to the hilt. I want to fill her and fuck her while she calls me *sissy, pussy, weak, bad boy*. While she whips me, spanks me, bites me with sharp little white teeth.

I close my eyes and try to focus. I try not to cave or move against her because that would be bad. It is the fourth slide and her breasts are rubbing against my chest. The blue silk of her blouse adds smooth pleasure to my dull pain. I thrust up without thinking, second nature when I'm hard.

"Oh...John. Bad boy. Bad John," Lucinda singsongs.

Goose bumps crop up along my skin. I shiver even though I'm sweating. She takes the clip off my nipple and the blood rushes in, a beautifully painful bliss that hurts in its own special way. The yellow lighter emerges so fast it could be sleight of hand. Orange flames jump to life and I watch her slide the narrow point of the clip—the part with the teeth—through the flame. "Oh, I can't—" I start.

"But I can," she finishes.

She blows on the now darkened metal, licks it for a moment, and I am horrified to hear it sizzle against her tongue. "Not too bad," she says and the jaws clamp down again, hot and bright. I give a little squeal and dance in my seat.

"Please! Please!"

Keep it on? Take it off? Let me go? Tie me tighter? Kiss-me-fuck-me-set-me-free? Fuck, even I don't know.

Lucinda traps my free nipple, the one that is still throbbing, between her fingernails. They are short milky half-moons at the end of her long tan fingers. She clamps harder and pain rears up with a vengeance. I focus on pushing my ass down into the seat. If I focus on pushing down, I will not pump up like a mindless animal seeking the heat of her pussy.

I have two different kinds of pain, and my brain somehow grows sharp and crystalline. The sounds of traffic, the smell of her shampoo, her breath on my face: it is all so intense I think I might cry. And my cock—how bad do I want to come right now? I think I would die to come.

She must be psychic. She leans in and kisses me, pulling me to her as much as she can manage. This levers me out and the rope gnaws at my already raw skin and I know I will have marks,

marks I will have to explain when I return home. I will deal with that later. She shimmies like live sex in my lap and then she is pulling me free. My cock is hot and ready in her hand—her hand that feels like the softest moleskin. I consciously push down. I will not thrust up. It will ruin everything. The pain from my nipples is slinking across my skin. Heat floods my chest and my breath hitches when she runs a finger along my tip. "God."

"Not now. Pray later," she says and sinks down onto me in one molten plunge.

I pray I will not come right then and there.

Those fingernails bite, bite, bite. The jaw of her hair clip is no longer hot but it is still excruciating. She shoves her free hand in my hair as she fucks me. She pulls and I see stars in the dark car: green, yellow, purple. "I'm going to come, lover boy," she growls. I believe her because she is so terribly gorgeously wet. Her body clutches at me. Her tempo is insane. She is a whirling dervish and I am so close, right there. But I won't let go, not yet.

She comes, crying out, head thrown back like something primitive, untamed. She digs her fingernails in and I feel the hot run of blood. She's cut me. She's cut me! The excitement is chaotic in my chest. "Come, good boy. Come, John. It's okay."

So I do. I let go and I finally, blissfully am allowed to fuck up into her as I shoot. "I'm sorry!" is the last thing I say.

I don't know why I'm sorry. Or what I'm sorry for. But I say it every time. Maybe I am sorry that I like them so much: the ones who bring me pain.

She begins to untie me and here it comes, the sadness. It happens every time it ends. "You live here?" Lucinda whispers.

"No. I'm here on business. Just a few days." I am growing flaccid inside of her but I still relish the tight wet feel of her.

"You at the hotel up the street?"

I nod and rub my chafed, nearly bloody wrists. "On Thomas Street."

"I'll come with you," she says and works her skirt down. We reassemble ourselves as best we can.

I find my keys and move to start the car. Lucinda stills my hand. "Oh, no. Scoot over, John, I'm driving."

I maneuver over the armrest and buckle up. I can't help but smile as she cranks the engine and turns on the headlights. She is the real deal.

THE SALSA BAR

Jolene Hui

Every time I think about that night, I smile. That was the drunkest I'd ever been. Two vodka Cokes in a salsa bar in Nice, France, and I was gone. Daniel, the bus driver, had eagerly gone to the bar to retrieve my drinks. I bought my first one, he my second. My mother was sucking on a Marlboro Red and laughing with the person next to her—some guy with long tangled hair. She was a fox. Me, at twenty-one, and her at thirty-seven—we looked like a couple of friends out for a night of fun.

My long brown hair was done in waves, and my mom's slightly darker hair was straight and sleek. We'd been travelling around France with a tour group. It was only fifteen of us and most of the crowd was middle-aged. We were the young hot ones and we were taking advantage of it.

Our tour guide, Olivier, was a hot Frenchman with tanned skin and light brown hair brushed with highlights. His accent was thick and his gestures swift. His greenish eyes looked at me intently every time I stepped onto the bus. His fingertips grazed my thighs often. When we got to Nice, mere hours before we went to the salsa bar, my mom and I walked up to our room and looked outside of our window. The buildings outside were different colors, the shutters inconsistently opened and closed.

"Oh, my god, look at the bathroom!" she shrieked. The bathroom was essentially a big shower, with a toilet and a sink. We laughed at it and plopped down on our beds. We could smell the ocean air from our window.

"Let's go get a drink," I suggested. Our group dinner was not until tomorrow night and I wanted to walk along the ocean.

We grabbed our purses and walked out the door. Downstairs in the lobby, we ran into Daniel. He was British but had spent most of his teenage years in the French countryside with some hippie group. That morning, he had told my mother something about some communist group he was involved in but I was too busy adoring Olivier's new green safari-looking hat. Olivier stood across the lobby from me, talking on his cell phone. He was always talking on his cell phone. I made eye contact with him. He smiled. I waited for him to hang up before I approached him. He grabbed me by the waist and kissed me on the cheek.

"Look what I have." He opened a little pocket on the side of his hat and pulled out a condom.

I giggled. "Wow, you're always prepared, aren't you?"

"It's the perfect-sized pocket for one."

"Maybe we could use it sometime?" I smiled and pulled him by the hand to where my mom and Daniel were talking about the political system in the United States.

I tore her away, promising to meet up with the guys later, and walked to the closest bar. I ordered a vodka martini and was presented with a regular glass filled with vodka.

"Oh, my god, it's straight," I said, sipping through a straw.

My mother drank a whiskey tonic. "Well, suck it down. I'm ready to go out salsa-ing!"

We sat outside at a table with the ocean just steps away. Boats were docked and large rocks marked the boundary between sand and pavement. The ocean air made our hair slightly crazy. Our trip though the French countryside had been wonderful. Neither of us had been out of the country before and this was truly a good bonding experience.

"I saw Olivier's special compartment," I told my mom. My head started to cloud.

"What?"

"He has this little pocket on his hat. It has a condom in it."

"A rubber?"

My mom preferred that term, which always made me laugh.

"Yes, mom, a rubber."

"Are you going to try it out?"

I slapped her on the arm.

"What? We're out of the country. You should really do something crazy like that."

How many mothers encouraged their daughters to sleep with their hot, hunky, tour guides? She was awesome. I sipped on my drink and thought about Olivier's eyes. He'd been touching me the whole tour—casual brushes on the knee, fingertips on my shoulder. It was like electricity being shot through my entire nervous system. The waves carried themselves through every bit of me and settled in my lower body. I sizzled just thinking about it. My lips were damp with alcohol when we started walking back to the hotel.

The guys were waiting where we left them. My mom went directly to Daniel and started blabbing. I could tell she was attracted to him. The thought of my mother trying to get in his pants was not something I wanted to think about, but

I was glad she was having a good time.

"Where are we going, Daniel?" I asked, breaking up their animated conversation. My mother was married, but I could tell she wanted a little spice in her life. I grabbed Olivier's hand and she grabbed Daniel's. Olivier's hand radiated heat. Butterflies dashed around in my stomach.

"The bar's not too far from here," said Daniel. "I go every time I'm here. I don't dance, but I love to listen to the band."

Olivier's hand moved to my lower back. We walked and talked along the way.

"So do you like salsa music usually?" I inquired, touching Olivier's arm.

"No, but I'd like to get your sexy body on the dance floor," he said softly into my ear.

My mom and Daniel were ahead of us. We were behind in the darkness. His lips moved closer to my ear. I could feel his breath on my neck.

The salsa bar was loud, and the music rang in my ears. Bright lights decorated the entire bar area and the band was dressed in zesty oranges, reds, and blues. There was a real actual disco ball above the dance floor.

Daniel set a drink in front of me as soon as I sat at the table. I paid him back for it. I was still buzzed from the drink earlier. The room was spinning in no time, the lights a kaleidoscope. Daniel set another drink in front of me and wouldn't accept my money this time. He and my mom sat at a table next to ours and looked at menus. She started talking to a guy with long hair next to her. Olivier led me to the dance floor and pressed his body to mine. In my liquor haze I pressed my lips to his. I had no idea how to salsa but our bodies seemed to move together seamlessly. His hands went to my waist and his hips swirled. I broke eye contact to see an older woman in spandex next to the stage moving to the music. She was precise in her movements and extremely sexual. It was like a dream, the music, the lights, the woman and her fuchsia lipstick, her short gray hair slicked back against her head. Olivier pulled me out the back door where we ended up on the rocky beach. He pulled me close like we had been inside. The music echoed outside and the soft tide mingled in to create a perfect soundtrack. I pulled apart to look at the ocean and noticed a tall blond man standing near us. His eyes were distant. He looked at the waves crashing. I got a rush of excitement when I realized I wondered what it would be like for him to join in. I wonder if he would. He was young, attractive, and looked lonely.

Olivier put his hands under my shirt and kissed my neck. I let him touch me how he wanted to. It felt fantastic. The smell of the ocean stuck to our skin. I didn't know if he was drunk, but it didn't really matter. With his lips tugging on my ear, he put us both down in the rocky sand. He was on top of me and I could feel his cock against my thigh. "Mmm," I murmured, reaching down to unzip his pants. I freed his cock and stroked it gently. I hardly noticed the sound of footsteps in the sand, as my grip tightened a bit on Olivier. I opened my eyes when I felt someone standing next to me. It was the blond.

No one said anything and I didn't freeze up at all. I was on vacation and it was time to do something like this. Olivier stopped what he was doing and looked up at the man. The man's pupils were large with excitement. I could see them burning in the darkness. He knelt down next to us in the sand. Olivier's hands were still on my breasts. He moved them to my waist, kissed me, gripped and moved me onto my hands and knees. He lifted my shirt up and kissed my lower back. I was facing the stranger. I arched my back and nudged Olivier's chest. He slid off my shiny black pants. I hadn't worn any underwear because I knew something like this would happen. I made eye contact with the stranger. He was still on his knees and looking down at me. Olivier licked my already wet pussy and stuck two fingers inside me while I stared into the stranger's eyes. His face was extremely masculine: a large nose with a ridge on it, and a strong jawline. His hair was short and slightly messy. He was wearing dress pants and a button-up shirt with the sleeves rolled up. I took note of every part of him while Olivier worked my pussy over. I panted and moaned softly. I didn't want to be too loud and bring attention to us outside. My hands and knees sunk into the sand.

I could hear the music from the club. When I closed my eyes, I could still see the lights. They bounced around on my eyelids.

"Time to open the compartment," Olivier said. I turned my head to see him getting the condom out of the pocket. I smiled and panted: my pussy wanted to be penetrated by his French cock. He opened the package up and slid the condom on. I turned back to face the stranger. By that time he had freed his dick from his pants. He nudged it softly against my nose without saying anything. Olivier shoved his cock inside of me. I squealed with pleasure and put my lips around the stranger's dick. They both pumped inside me. The stranger tasted mildly of sweat. His cock fit nicely into my mouth. And he was courteous—he didn't shove it down my throat. He was gentlemanly. Olivier gripped my waist and the stranger gripped my hair. I whimpered, the cock muffling any sounds that tried to escape.

I came hard, shoving my ass into Olivier, my cum drenching his pubic hair and dripping onto the sand. The stranger could tell I was getting off and shot his load hard into my mouth. I pulled away, somewhat ill prepared. His cum dripped from my lips.

Olivier pulled out, put his hand around my waist, and helped me stand up. I pulled my pants up and wiped my mouth with the back of my hand. The cum stuck to my lips, the taste salty and raw.

The stranger zipped himself into his pants, leaned over, kissed my cheek, and walked away.

I had sand on my hands and all over the knees of my pants. Olivier threw the condom away in a trash can. We walked back inside, my head still spinning.

"Where were you guys?" asked my mother, sucking on a cigarette.

"Dancing on the beach," I winked at her and she slapped me across the arm.

The old lady was still dancing by the stage. Olivier had his hand on my lower back. The lights were still surreal. When I was being fucked I didn't even notice my spinning head. But when I focused on the bright colors of the band, everything started to swirl. I needed to get out fast.

Daniel, my mother, Olivier, and I left the bar. Olivier and Daniel grabbed on to my arms and made sure I could walk. I was fine but I enjoyed having them on either side. My mother walked on Daniel's side.

"It's perfect weather, isn't it?" my mom asked.

"Yeah, it was beautiful outside...." I trailed off.

"Oh, when you were dancing?" She winked at me.

The guys dragged me back to the hotel and by the time we reached the door, I was feeling a little better.

"I'm going up," said my mom. "Don't stay out too late."

I had no idea what time it was.

"See you all tomorrow," Daniel said, and walked away behind my mother.

Olivier and I were left alone outside.

"I had a good time tonight." I smiled.

He held me around the waist. "I did, too. But now I have to fill the pocket again."

We laughed. He kissed my mouth and put his hands on my ass, slightly gripping.

"I'll see you tomorrow," he said, smacking my ass.

I took my dizzy ass up to my room to get some sleep before my day on the beach tomorrow. I licked my lips.

I knew that I'd never forget the beach in Nice.

FANNING THE FLAMES

Andrea Dale

Oh, *now* he'd done it.

Catriona had never been one for pitching fits, but so help her, right now she just wanted to stamp her foot and let out a nice cathartic scream of pure frustration.

But the last thing she wanted to see was the glittering amusement in Jake McGovern's dark eyes at her tantrum.

The last thing she wanted to see was, in fact, Jake McGovern.

"Good evening, Ms. Sullivan," he said, all suave and solid in his tuxedo, the bump of his gun not even visible. Unless that was a gun in his custom trousers, and she was reasonably sure he was storing something else entirely there.

She'd spent some quality time alone with her vibrator fantasizing about just what the bodyguard's cock might look like. And feel like…

"Take the night off, Jake," she said, indicating the front door of her soon-to-be-ex fiancé Timothy's Atlanta penthouse. "It's not that big a party."

"He asked me to look after you tonight," Jake said. He leaned against the wall, but his body was anything but relaxed.

Dammit. She was screwed.

Timothy, her fiancé, was cheating on her. In fact, she knew damn well his current "business trip" wasn't about business. Apparently he thought he was being discreet, or he thought she was stupid (or probably, both), but the upshot was simple: she was outta here.

She had no interest in confronting him or creating a scene. He was disgustingly wealthy and extremely powerful, and he'd make her life hell if she did. Nope, she was just going to gather up the expensive jewelry and designer clothes and a few electronic toys—all things he'd given her, nothing more—and take off.

The plan was simple: She'd make an appearance at the Morelli's charity ball, then slip out, and no one would be the wiser for several days. Her bags were packed and in the trunk of her Mercedes SUV.

Now Timothy had screwed everything up, via Jake.

There was no arguing with Jake, either. Hell, she'd figure something out. "Fine," she said. "Let's go."

"You look lovely tonight," he commented as he held out her wrap. His dark blue eyes caressed her curves as assuredly as if he'd used his hands—she felt as if he had, at any rate.

She knew she looked fabulous, in a flirty red chiffon dress with a plunging neckline and variegated hem. Timothy hated red. The outfit represented her bid for freedom.

Jake's visual assessment left her feeling almost naked. Naked except for her scarlet garter belt and matching thong and spike heels…

She clenched her thighs, resisting the unbidden shiver of desire. Focus. She had to focus.

She insisted they take the Mercedes, and he insisted he drive, and she let him. Better not to deviate too far from routine. On the way, she pondered how to ditch Jake. A former Navy SEAL—or was it Marine? She couldn't remember—he had all the training and skills, and then some. Nothing escaped him.

But she would have to.

The Morelli's had a string quartet; catering by one of Atlanta's most exclusive restaurants; and a guest list that included two movie stars, three top athletes, and numerous politicians. Champagne flowed from an ice fountain. Catriona allowed herself one glass, for show.

She mingled, exchanging platitudes and polite laughter, trying to lose herself in the crowd. But no matter where she went, Jake was always there, watching her. She didn't even have to look around to know. She could feel his gaze on her, hot and unyielding.

Kind of like how his cock would feel when...

Stop. Just stop it. She had to keep her eyes on the prize.

She licked lips suddenly gone dry, and out of the corner of her eye saw Jake stand a little straighter.

Catriona glanced around. She didn't see a threat, so Jake had to have been reacting to her. Oh, ho, is that so? Just to check, she trailed her fingers down the low neckline of her dress, along the visible curve of her breast.

Jake coughed, shifted his stance. If she'd been closer, she strongly suspected she'd see a nice swelling in his pants.

Aha. A new plan. She'd distract him, she decided. She'd flirt and tease, and when the blood was no longer in his brain, she'd slip away.

She walked toward him with a deliberate sway in her hips, stood just a little too close. "I hate that you don't get to have any fun. Can I get you a drink?"

"I don't drink when I'm on duty," he said.

"Something nonalcoholic, then."

"I'm fine."

He didn't sound fine. He sounded like he was gritting his teeth. She glanced down. Excellent. Time to ramp it up a notch.

"Whoops." She dropped her little beaded handbag.

They both went down to retrieve it. Rather than an accidental bumping of heads, though, she timed it so that Jake's face essentially ended up in her cleavage.

They both froze for a moment, so close she could feel his warm breath on her flesh. The sensation sent a tingle to her core.

She shifted a little, giving him a clearer view down her dress, before slowly rising to her feet, deliberately and evocatively brushing against him as she did.

"Thank you," she said, taking the purse from him. "Now, you really should get some water and cool down. I'm going to the ladies' room, and you certainly can't follow me there."

She felt him watching her as she sashayed off.

Dammit. The bathroom window was too small to climb out of. She pursed her lips, considering her options.

There was a parlor at the back of the house, with French doors opening onto a back patio. It was the only other option she could try that wouldn't mean she'd have to cross the ballroom again, where Jake would see her.

A few more minutes, and then she'd be free.

The parlor was dark. She eased open the French door. Sultry night air caressed her face.

"Just where do you think you're going?"

She managed to stifle a shriek. "Oh, I—I was just getting some air."

Leather creaked as he reached up and clicked on a reading lamp. He was sitting in an armchair, one leg crossed over the other. Even though his eyes were in shadow, his piercing gaze made her shiver.

"I don't think so, Catriona." His fingers drummed against the arm of the chair. "Tell me the truth."

Okay, time for Plan B. She didn't really have a Plan B, so she improvised. She'd throw herself on his mercy....

It wasn't a great plan, but it was a plan.

"Timothy's cheating on me, so I'm leaving him," she said. "Tonight. Will you help me?"

He watched her, fingers still drumming, for interminable minutes. Finally, he said, "On one condition."

She assumed he meant money. "Name it."

He crooked his finger. "Come here."

Uh-oh. Mouth dry again, she stepped forward, stopping just before the chair.

He watched her, silent and menacing and undeniably sexy.

She knew what he wanted. She wanted to pretend he didn't, just as she wanted to pretend her thighs weren't weak and her heart wasn't pounding and she'd never thought about this before when she thought about Jake and his strength and power.

She wanted to deny how much she craved this. Her cheeks flushed as red as she guessed her ass would become, and the shiver of humiliation only made her grow slicker.

Her breath hitched as she arranged herself across his lap, feeling his muscled thighs tighten as she settled on them.

She hung her head, glad her hair hid her blushes when he drew up her skirt. She swore she could feel the heat of his gaze on her bare flesh. As much as she tried not to, she clenched against it.

"How long have you been planning on leaving Timothy?" Jake asked.

What? Confused, she said, "Th—three weeks."

"Twenty-one days. That's twenty-one smacks."

Oh, god. No. She wanted to tell him she'd estimated, that it had been less time than that, but she was sure that would get her into far more trouble. Plus she could barely think, barely count, and there was no time, because she felt his body shift and his hand came down on her defenseless bottom.

Her head reared up, but she caught her scream and muffled it into a breathy squeal just as the second slap landed. She couldn't make noise or the other guests would hear. But how could they not hear the gunshot cracks?

Pain flared with every spank, with barely enough time to fade, mutate into heat, before the next stinging blow. She told herself she wouldn't cry, but he was relentless, hitting the same spots so the sharp hurt intensified.

Her ass felt swollen, fiery hot, and so did her cleft. Her thong cut into her crotch, digging against her clit, which throbbed and trembled the more he added to the pain.

She tried to wriggle, but it added to her desperate arousal, and she knew that if she asked him to stop, he wouldn't help her sneak out.

Or, worse, he'd punish her even more.

It was that thought that did her in.

Catriona had no idea how close they'd gotten to twenty-one. If it was soon, then she might not...

Oh, god, oh, god.

The orgasm built and rolled through her and smashed into her just as Jake's hand smashed down again, and she screamed into her fist, unable to stop the contractions or the sweet damned pain.

She thought she heard him say "Oh, *good* girl," and she bowed her head and swore she'd never look at him again, even as a final betraying tremor pulsed through her.

Jake flipped her skirt back down, and even the flimsy chiffon felt heavy and rough against her puffy, tenderized cheeks. He helped her to her feet, steadying her when her weak legs threatened to give way. Confused, she turned to him, wondering if he wanted a blow job, but he shook his head and said, "We'd better get going."

Catriona turned for the French doors, but he took her arm.

"Can't go that way," he said. "There's a locked, alarmed gate on either side of the house, and an eight-foot fence in the back. We've got to go through the front."

If the humiliation of being soundly spanked by Jake and of coming to a sobbing orgasm from the spanking hadn't been humiliation enough, now she had to parade through the party, sure that everyone knew her ass was the same glowing scarlet as her dress.

At least he let her duck into the ladies' room first to repair her makeup. But nothing could cover the flush on her cheeks and the brightness in her eyes, and she didn't have time to clean between her legs, so her wet thighs slipped and slid against each other and she could smell her pungent juices.

Horrifyingly, all of it made her want to come again.

"Catriona? Not leaving us so soon?" Angela Morelli appeared from nowhere.

"Ms. Sullivan isn't feeling well," Jake said. He didn't stop walking, so Angela practically had to walk backward.

"Please give my best to your husband," Catriona managed. "I'm sorry."

"Oh, no, I'm sorry. I'll call you tomorrow," Angela said as she was left in their wake. Catriona didn't even have the strength to wave.

* * *

She let Jake drive again. She didn't even ask where he was going, as long as it was away from the penthouse.

"I have to ask this." She cleared her throat. "Why did you go turncoat tonight? That doesn't seem like you."

"I didn't."

"But Timothy hired you…"

Jake glanced at her, a small smile on his lips. "I said he *asked* me to work tonight. I turned him down. I knew he was cheating on you, and I wanted no part of it. But then I decided to come with you tonight, and tell you the truth afterward."

Her pussy clenched, a delicious tremor rocking her sex. "So…you would have helped me anyway. You didn't have to blackmail me by…"

"Say it, Catriona." His voice brooked no argument.

She almost couldn't form the words. "By making me lie across your lap. Oh, god." Her voice cracked as a fresh wave of humiliation washed through her.

"No, I didn't have to," he admitted, not a shred of remorse in his voice. "But the opportunity was too delicious to pass up. You can't tell me you didn't enjoy it, Catriona." His voice dipped low. "You know you did."

Moisture, heat, pressure welled up between her legs again, sudden and strong. Her tender ass throbbed harder. She betrayed herself by squirming in the leather seat.

"And when we get to a motel, we'll explore just what else you enjoy."

Oh, god…

ON A HOT TIN ROOF

I. K. Velasco

There was that harsh disinfectant smell—an illusion of clean. There were still pockets of dirt around the cracks and crevices of the tile. There was the steep staircase with the rickety rail, the heavy unlocked door, the rasp of rusty hinges, the harsh sunlight, and the wall of wet heat. Past the threshold, there was the blacktop, the rooftop garden, and the plastic kiddie pool, blue with yellow ducks on the edges. One of the sides was tilted down, the side where her head weighted the pillow polyester. And she was there, of course, wearing only an inch of water and a wayward grin.

I stood with my hands in my pockets. My palms felt sweaty, like the beads of moisture on her naked skin.

"On the roof," I said. Her eyebrows arched.

"I'm hot." Obvious. "A/C's busted. It's like an oven inside my loft. Baking my bones."

"Feel good out here?"

"Of course. Are you going to join me?" There was that

dangerous tone and the matching look. I turned away from her.
I couldn't give in. Not quite yet.

I looked at the view, the three-tiered urban tectonic layers—
hazy blue, after an acid rain sky on the top; on the bottom, criss-
crossed alleys and boulevards; and in the middle, the blocks of
brownstone, steel, and skyscraper, each with a matching rooftop,
just like the one I was standing on. There were thousands of
them, stacked on top of us. How many people inhabited those
rooftops right at this moment, escaping (embracing) the sun?
How many people could see me? Could see her? I swallowed my
heart into my stomach.

There was always that. That feeling. That possibility. That
danger. Something that I never thought I would need. Rather,
she needed it. And I needed her.

"You're scared," she said.

"Maybe."

"It is high. Twenty stories."

"You know it's not the height."

There was the time when she'd handcuffed herself to the
bookshelves at the library, the 58th Street branch. I found her
on the fifth floor, medieval history section. I rocked her against
the shelves, shaking the whole row as the leather-bound books
clapped the linoleum. Both hands were bound. I always wondered
how she'd accomplished that by herself.

There was the time at the Met. While the members of the
board and the honored sponsors had cocktails and hors d'oeuvres
in the main hall, I fucked her in the Asian Art wing. We did it
under the watchful eye of the Standing Buddha, fifth century
Gupta period. The mottled red limestone matched the flush of
her skin.

There was the time when she'd followed me home, and I'd
found her on the Queens West. The subway car stayed empty

until Canal Street, but her eyes stayed focused on the windows and the whispering doors, looking for those strangers, for the danger. Her hands clutched the bar above, her craving apparent by the stretched, distended muscles of her arms.

There were those times and many others. But this wasn't the same. There had always been that inky gloom, some blanket of protection in the shadow of night. In the heat of this summer day, there was the luminous glare, the harsh radiation. These are the sources of danger—the light that eats the shadows, exposing reality within. I felt safer in the dark.

I finally looked at her. She looked at me. She was anxious. I could tell from the tightness in the corners of her mouth. Her eyes stayed clear, glassy black lakes. I had delayed enough. She wouldn't ask again. She didn't have to.

I undressed and as the cloth released my skin, there was that perilous exposure—that heat touching the fleshy surface and everything inside. I shivered.

I stood in the inch of water, my feet between her legs. She twisted up toward me, her palms on my hips. Her mouth was there, too fast. She was always this way—quick to act, eager to consume. I pulled away, clutched her shoulders, and moved underneath. She hovered, the wave of her hair brushing my chest. There was the harsh sunlight, mercurial incandescence surrounding the glow of her silhouette. I closed my eyes, crushed her mouth. She tasted like dynamite. There was the burn there, the fever of her softness surrounding my length, swallowing me into her.

"Mmm…it's hot out here," she said.

I opened my eyes. The haze swam into focus on her wayward smile. Not directed at me. I followed her gaze and watched the stranger wave from the next rooftop.

HOT OFF
THE PRESS

Thomas S. Roche

Deirdre already had the first line written before she even had her clothes off. It popped into her head when she looked around the fantastically opulent bedroom of the hotel suite: *Crass Faster's room at the Tall Tree Inn wasn't as nice as I expected.* She was thinking ironically, but she didn't have time to write the punch line in her head, which would have gone something like *It was only the nicest fucking hotel room I've ever seen,* because she simply had to get her clothes off.

For tonight she'd strayed far from her usual jeans and a tight T-shirt; she was all decked out like the kind of slut, she figured, who went backstage at a Crass Faster concert to fuck the performer. She wriggled out of her impossibly short plaid schoolgirl miniskirt, kicked off her high-heeled shoes, took off her garter belt and fishnet stockings, and the almost ludicrously infinitesimal black mesh thong that had been crawling up her ass all fucking evening. She piled it all on a nearby Danish Modern chair in a rumpled lump that reeked of cigarettes, weed, liquor, and sex, her purse atop it. One thing she did *not* remove was her Crass Faster T-shirt, because she thought it would be kind of hot for the guy to come in here and fuck her while she was wearing it, and in any event she didn't want him to miss the point she was making by spreading herself on his bed—that she was a fan. I mean, she thought it would already be pretty obvious, but why take chances? Her career was at stake.

Deirdre wondered if maybe she ought to slip into the shower for a quick rinse. She decided that was out of the question; Crass Faster was probably on his way up. He could enter the hotel room at any moment, and she wanted to be ready. Besides, she didn't want to take off her dog collar. Deirdre checked herself in the giant mirror that covered one whole wall of the bedroom suite. Yup, she looked like a slut, all right. Naked from the waist down, big tits spilling out of her T-shirt, shaved, collared, painted—she checked the traits off on her mental checklist; yes, yes, she looked like a whore. Mission accomplished. She'd already touched up her makeup in the bathroom at the after party, but she figured an encounter with Crass Faster was worth a little more cherry-musk lip gloss, so she fetched some from her purse and slicked up her lips till they glowed and smacked of sickly sweet sex. Oh, she couldn't wait to smear that sickly sweet sex up and down Crass Faster's hard prong and email Courtney the snapshots on motherfucking Eye-Fi. She was getting wet just thinking about it: that'd show the bitch.

Deirdre put her camera and tape recorder on the night-stand and crawled onto the bed, thrilling at the feel of the silky comforter. She stretched out on the bed naked except for her dog collar and about six pounds of makeup. Tasting cherry musk, she pouted at the door and practiced spreading her legs.

Deirdre was not naturally a slut. She eschewed romantic relationships in favor of furthering her writing career. She was known across Redwood College as the girl who'd been in every issue of every campus publication since she'd arrived at Redwood three and a half years ago. She'd taken on the school newspaper first—natch. In the first issue of Deirdre's first semester they published her letter to the editor about how there were no sanitary napkins in the dorm bathrooms the first day of school, and Deirdre had never looked back since.

Ravenous for publication, she'd written journalism, fiction, political commentary, poetry, even song lyrics so she could be in last semester's music department broadsheet. She'd even taken a crash course in French when she'd found out that department was putting out a Francophile literary magazine; she'd lost a semester's worth of sleep just to get her short poem *"Lirez-vous mon écriture, Pierre?"* into the Frenchy rag.

Though by all accounts she was far from unattractive and, as her mom was embarrassingly fond of saying, she certainly had quite a rack on her, Deirdre's interest in sex was primarily a literary interest. She would never have conceded that she lost her virginity solely for the purpose of writing about it for the controversial campus erotica publication *Evening Dew*, but that actually was the sad fact. And here she was, tarted up like some rock and roll bimbo, practicing spreading her legs on Crass Faster's hotel bed strictly because of Courtney Capricious.

That wasn't even Courtney's real name, of course, which was a total death sentence for any respect Deirdre might have felt for the girl—Deirdre considered pseudonyms cowardly and, much worse, cheesy. In the very last semester of Deirdre's Redwood College career, Courtney, a fine arts major, had somehow—somehow!—secured partial funding from the lit department for her publication *Hot Off the Press*, which would collect real-life student encounters with rock stars.

This thing was guaranteed controversy; Christ, when this

fucker hit the stands the Religious Right in this state were going to shit themselves. Deirdre half planned to make the call to the local wing-nut radio station herself! Deirdre saw outraged newspaper editorials in Courtney's future, coverage in the national media, radio spots, maybe even television—we're talking debate in the state legislature, damn it, a new bill regulating the content of university-funded publications; it made Deirdre's head swim! How Courtney'd convinced the school administration to fund such a project in the first place was utterly beyond everyone; Deirdre thought, unkindly, that *Ms. Capricious' famous pierced and painted lips were clearly working their magic on certain private aspects of school administrators' anatomy,* which is exactly what she planned to write in a confessional piece after the fact, possibly denouncing the publication as a decadent bourgeois attempt at creating sexual adventure to quantify the alienation of their generation from the sociopolitical process—if Marxism was still trendy by then.

The problem was that *Hot Off the Press*'s partial lit department funding meant it was technically an official campus publication. If Deirdre's writing didn't make it in, it would break her perfect record. The official status could be argued, but Deirdre didn't want to spend the rest of her life making that case to herself, so she intended to be in that ToC if it was the last fucking thing she ever did.

But Courtney Capricious was less than fond of Deirdre, and had told her in no uncertain terms that she considered Deirdre to be a stuck-up kiss-ass. And this after Deirdre, right after hearing about *Hot Off the Press*'s green-lighting, had shown up in Courtney's office carrying flowers, chocolates, and the latest Perky Balderdash bootleg from Vomit Records downtown! What did she have to do to win this bitch over?

Clearly not just write a good piece; she'd already written

four of them, and Courtney had bounced them all. There'd been Deirdre's fantasy about making it with Jimi Hendrix and Kurt Cobain in a brothel in heaven, her six-page prose poem about Jonny Buckland's fingers, and a lengthy dissertation on what Pink's haircut meant to female empowerment. No, no, and no—Courtney insisted that all stories be real first-person sexual encounters with rock stars. Deirdre had finally caved and blown Jake McKendrick, the singer from Saddest, the ever-popular campus emo band. She'd done it for the sole purpose of writing about it, with clinical detachment and pausing to jot a few details on her reporter's notebook halfway through, which Jake didn't even notice because he was too busy talking about his ex-girlfriend Bethany (about whom most of his songs were written) and how he really believed they were meant to be together. It was like he was writing fucking emo lyrics while she was going down on him—this was memoir gold, damn it!—and she put every detail into the article. But when she turned the piece in, Courtney gleefully informed Deirdre that she already had not one but two stories about fucking Jake McKendrick, and both of them had him blathering on about Bethany while in flagrante delicto. Deirdre's story, she was told, didn't rate—she hadn't even boned the sad fucker. The funny thing was that nobody had ever met Bethany; Jake, suspiciously, claimed to have burned all his pictures of her, which was kind of strange for a guy with 4,700 pictures in his Flickr stream of himself with his shirt off looking sad. Clearly, there was more than one Redwood College coed who would appreciate knowing if the intimacy she'd shared with Jake was just a squirt or six in the ocean of tears coaxed from him by some slutty siren of emo despair—or if the guy was, in fact, deranged.

But Courtney sneered at Deirdre's enthusiastic offer of an investigative journalism piece called "Who is Bethany? A

Jake McKendrick Fan Looks for Some Answers in the Tangle of Sad Songs and Groupie Sex." "First person, Deirdre," said Courtney. "It has to be first person. And it better be good, no more small-town losers like Jake. We're getting close to deadline, DeeDee. You'd better bag Keith Richards in the next twelve days, or you're going to break your perfect record." Courtney always called her DeeDee, or more accurately "dD," when she was trying to piss Deirdre off; it was both a diminutive reference to her name and a skanky jab at Deirdre's cup size.

That particular day, Courtney had been wearing a Crass Faster T-shirt, two sizes too small with the sleeves and neckline ripped out.

"Isn't he coming to town soon?" snapped Deirdre.

Courtney laughed hysterically. "dD, if you can fuck Crass Faster you've got a guaranteed slot in *Hot Off the Press*," she said nastily. "I'll even put you first." She started laughing. "Hell, I know you're not that much of a slut, dD, so I'll even make it easy for you—all you have to do is blow him." She cackled. "But I want pictures."

"Oh, I'll get you pictures," said Deirdre, her voice ice cold.

The rest, as they say, was history.

That's why Deirdre ended up spread out on a king-sized bed at the Tall Tree Inn, the only hotel in San Isidore that even *had* a Presidential Suite. *How* she ended up there was a bit hazier, not because she was liquored up (she didn't drink much—her only drunken binge had been for a first-person cautionary piece on student drinking) but because there had been so many hand jobs and blow jobs involved just getting into Crass's room. Deirdre didn't mind any of them. In fact, she'd rather enjoyed the experience, having had very little opportunity for no-strings-attached sex in a college as small as Redwood, since she had a strict rule against sleeping with anyone who could not advance her career. Besides, that third roadie had been fairly cute, and the second security guard had even thoughtfully offered to get her off with a vibrator he had stashed in his jacket pocket, which she had certainly appreciated. She'd declined cheerfully, wanting to save her sexual energy for Crass, whom she planned to fuck cross-eyed and bowlegged. She'd enjoyed all the fooling around enough to get pretty worked up; by the time she got her hands on Crass she was really going to go to town.

After her numerous encounters of the evening, she'd made several mental notes, however. First, next time she'd touch up her makeup only after the last blow job of the evening, or at least the last blow job before she actually met the rock star. The amount of makeup was perfect, though; heavy enough to look like a complete whore, and then just pile on some more. The shave job was most appreciated by the one roadie who'd so very much wanted to go down on her; in fact, it had felt so good she'd had to wrestle off her own orgasm, and had faked it in consideration for the guy's feelings, since he really was very good with that tongue. Next time she'd definitely trim her nails a bit shorter; that poor backup percussionist with the spandex pants was going to have a nasty scratch on his ball sac, and if her nails had been properly trimmed she would have fingered the drummer's girlfriend a little while they were making out, which probably would have gotten her in the door even faster. And next time, she decided, she'd go for the ratted-out, freshly-fucked slut hair to begin the evening with, since the neat, calculated businesslike goth-chick bob she'd chosen had ended up a rat's-nest mess—she was Robert Smith, here, spread and horny on Crass Faster's hotel room bed.

Deirdre heard the door opening. Her heart pounded. She'd been practicing spreading her legs for the better part of an hour by then, and as a figure stumbled into the room she realized she couldn't decide whether to spread or cross. She decided to spread—best to leave nothing to the imagination. She propped herself up and stuck out her tits and heard the torn neckline of her Crass Faster T-shirt go rrrrrrrrrrip!, which would have been kind of a turn-on if she hadn't been distracted by the large number of people spilling into the room, none of them Crass Faster. There were two, no three: two women, one man, all stumbling into the bedroom making out, feeling each other up, and ripping each others' clothes off. And more were coming, spilling into the room like somebody'd opened the doors of a late-night groupie asylum.

"Ho-ly *shit*," said Deirdre, not that anyone could hear her over the laughing and stumbling. There, in a *major* state of some serious effin' *en dishabille*, was Courtney. Tangled up with two girls and a kilt-wearing transvestite, she was shedding clothes as she came toward the bed. By the time she spotted Deirdre, Courtney was half-undressed, her skirt down around her knees, her Crass Faster shirt ripped to shreds, and her B-cup tits hanging out of a push-up bra. "Don't I know you?" burbled Courtney drunkenly as she stumbled onto the bed and planted her lips on Deirdre's. Deirdre tried to say something, but Courtney's tongue was wriggling its way into her mouth, tasting of Jack Daniels, cloves, pot, and—wow, that was interesting, apparently Deirdre was *not* Courtney's first woman of the night.

Deirdre only recognized the flavor from having tasted her own juices once a day for thirty days, for a now mildly famous article in *Redwood Health Review*.

"Courtney," hissed Deirdre when her editor—my god, how kinky was *that*?—let her up for air. "It's me, Deirdre!"

"Deirdre?" said Courtney brightly. "Oh, I do know you! Hi Deirdre, how's it going? Did you fuck Crass yet? I hear he's got the *best cock.*" Her hands found Deirdre's breasts and started fondling them through the shirt as she kissed Deirdre. "You're hot, Deirdre," said Courtney in the short distance her lips spent moving between Deirdre's mouth and her breasts, and Deirdre gasped a little as Courtney began to suck on her tits through the T-shirt.

"I've always thought you had the *best* tits," slurred Courtney. "Can I take this off?" She ripped the T-shirt unceremoniously, said loudly, "Oops!" and giggled.

Courtney began nuzzling Deirdre's tits, licking and sucking them as Deirdre wrestled with her conscience. Courtney was royally fucked up and everything, clearly not in her right mind. Deirdre really shouldn't take advantage of her. On the other hand, if she *didn't* show concern for her sister journalist and hustle the drunken slut into a cab downstairs, one of two things would happen; either Deirdre was guaranteed—*guaranteed!*— top billing in *Hot Off the Press*, or Courtney wouldn't remember a thing, and it would be as if nothing ever happened.

Deirdre reached for her camera.

"I'm sorry I was a bitch to you," said Courtney drunkenly. "You're just such a stacked little snatch, do you know what it's like trying to compete with knockers like these, Deirdre? My god, look at them! They're like a force of nature." Deidre pointed the camera and started shooting. "Ooh, we're making a porno now? I'm ready for my close-up, Mister...um...sleazy...porn...guy... girl...whatever." Courtney ripped what was left of the Crass Faster T-shirt all the way off of Deirdre's tits and began to suckle hungrily. Courtney had nice soft lips and it actually would have felt pretty good if Deirdre hadn't been busy getting a few choice shots of her own tits with Courtney's lips planted on them, and then distracted scanning the room for Crass Faster, who was nowhere to be seen in the steadily growing crowd. Someone in the tangle of bodies toward the end of the bed removed Courtney's skirt, and Courtney wrapped herself around Deirdre, sucking and fondling and making out. Courtney was now stark naked except for these knee-high pointy-toed shiny rock-and-roll slut boots. Some '80s boy was all over them, licking and sucking Courtney's shiny boots while a ratted-out Pamela Anderson clone undid his belt. Courtney started slurping her way drunkenly down Deirdre's belly, her tongue swirling wildly as the guy began really making love to her boots. Deirdre's eyes went wide as Courtney looked up at her from between her legs and said, "Didn't know I was a big lesbo, did you?" then giggled a little and planted her mouth on Deirdre's shaved puss, her tongue working with such fantastic expertise that Deirdre let out a sudden shocked gasp of pleasure.

It felt so fucking good, in fact, that Deirdre could barely work the shutter as her pleasure mounted. "Get my good side," giggled Courtney, her big dark eyes gazing up at the camera as she pulled back just far enough to let Deirdre shoot twenty fast pics in Sport Mode, Courtney's pretty face and that skilled tongue working visibly against Deirdre's bare puss. After that, it was all blurry and streaky because even with the flash Deirdre couldn't hold the camera still, it felt so fucking good. Courtney had managed to sit on '80s boy's face and no longer seemed to care about her good side. She buried her face eagerly between Deirdre's spread thighs and slurped for all she was worth. The piercing in her tongue was stroking smooth and hard against Deirdre's clit: damn, that felt good. Deirdre was starting not to care if she even *got* a byline on this piece, maybe it was getting filthy enough that she really ought to consider a pseudo—

There!! There he was, just inches away from the bed, his belt half-undone, a clove cigarette in one hand and a bottle of twenty-year-old Glenn Caith in the other. *There, goddamn it!*

"Excuse me!" she hissed to Courtney, and wrenched herself out of the naked editor's fervent embrace just enough to get a grip on the belt buckle on the bulging leather pants swaying in front of her at the edge of the bed; she pulled him close while Courtney looked up and pouted, her red lipstick smeared indelicately all over her face. Courtney wriggled after Deirdre and '80s boy after Courtney, and in a moment everyone was piled on top of everyone, '80s boy slurping and fingering Courtney while Courtney's fingers, two or maybe three of them, worked into Deirdre to match the motion of her tongue on Deirdre's surging clit. God, that felt fucking good, but not half as good as it felt to get Crass Faster's leather pants open and reach in and pull his hard cock out and plant her mouth on it, slurping her way up the shaft and swirling her tongue around the head, sweeping her freshly-fucked hair out of the way before pointing the camera and smiling.

She heard him mumble around his clove in a heavy Liverpool accent: "Annie fucking Leibovitz here, make sure you get me good side, will you, Annie? Blimey!" Which was kind of funny because wasn't Crass Faster from San Jose? Fuck it, she didn't care. She had a limited number of moments to get the perfect shot. Crass seemed less puzzled than she might have expected, to have this girl polishing his knob while she tried to get a shot with her face, his cock, and his face, which seemed to be next to impossible. It would have been only slightly easier if she could have rolled over, but when she tried that Courtney pinned her down and said, "Oh, for fuck's sake, Deirdre, I get it, you're blowing him, you're sucking off Crass Faster, you've got the fucking byline, okay?"

The words were music to her ears. Courtney's tongue was working again, her fingers deep inside her, and Deirdre let out a long, low sigh as she surrendered to her pleasure. The camera dropped from her grasp and she rose swiftly toward orgasm on Courtney's skilled tongue and hand, her own hand working Crass's cock up and down while she worked the head.

"Aw, so you're a writer as well as a photographer," purred Crass. "Keep doing that and I'll give you an *exclusive*, you slaggy little minx."

That's when she came, hard. Deirdre went all hot and buttery inside, pleasure suffusing her—*an exclusive*! Her orgasm was still riding high, Courtney's tongue working its magic as Deirdre tasted the first salty spurt of precome. Courtney wasn't far behind; she rode the '80s boy's face while Crass let out a long string of pleased obscenities, coming deep in Deirdre's throat. He was still doing the Liverpool accent, but it was faltering and got kind of half-Southern by the time he finished.

She was already writing the closing sentence in her head as she caressed Crass's softening, pink cock with her tongue, tasting cherry musk.

Then he came, and I came, we all came, she thought rapturously. *We all fucking came, like, all over the fucking place. It was hot.*

It certainly wasn't Deirdre's best prose, but there'd be plenty of time for a second draft.

SCORCHED

Janine Ashbless

M ax leaned over the gearshift to give her a kiss on the cheek. "Bye, love."

Emerald, one eye on the rearview mirror, smiled. "Bye. Have a good one."

"Yeah. Thanks for the lift." He opened the passenger-side door and a muffled railway announcement was audible over the commuter murmur and the traffic. Max hesitated. "You're going shopping?"

"Yes. Might have lunch with Jessica, if she's in town."

He nodded. "Pick me up the new Eisler thriller, will you?"

Emerald blinked. "Okay."

"Thanks. See you tonight, love." His hand descended briefly onto her thigh; half grope, half pat. "Love you."

"Love you too." She didn't drive off immediately despite the cars massing behind hers, waiting for her space. She watched Max's ginger-gold curls and lean arse disappear through the station doors, the swing of the satchel on his shoulder casually graceful. He was cute: after three years together she still found a furtive pleasure in watching him. She was so lucky to have Max as her boyfriend; she knew that. "Crap," she said to herself as she put the car into gear.

How annoying that he'd asked her to buy a book: now she really would have to go shopping instead of turning the car round and heading back to their flat. And this on her day off, with Greg probably still asleep in bed. It couldn't be helped, though. And, she thought as she set off in search of a parking garage, there were possibilities involved in shopping.

Two hours later she was walking through her front door with the book—and a new set of lingerie. Bra and panties were both a bold sunshine yellow, trimmed with black flowers. She'd bought them in a boutique in town, then slipped into a café washroom to change. The bra was cut to enhance her cleavage and the knickers were high-legged, tanga-style, with no cloth over the swell of her bum at all; her bare cheeks were framed by narrow bands of black peonies that emphasized the smooth sweet roundness of her bottom. Clasping her thighs were broad bands of matching flowers at the top of sheer black hold-up stockings. Emerald was taut with excitement as she slipped the key into the lock, dropped her bags in the hall, and walked through into the apartment.

Greg was in the living room, watching a World War Two documentary on the History Channel; he worked entirely online and kept erratic hours, and though it was sometimes hard to believe he worked at all, he actually earned more than either of his flatmates. He'd breakfasted and showered, judging by the empty cereal bowl at his feet and the fact he was wearing only a towel. He cast her a lazy look as she walked in.

"Hi, doll."

"Hi." Her stomach felt full of butterflies, her panties full of butter. The smell of shower gel hanging in the air promised clean damp skin.

"You took a long time." Greg was blockier than Max and had dark hair cut like a rug. His skin was tanned, though not from outdoor living—Max was the keen rambler but Greg merely liked to lie on the flat roof and catch the summer rays while he meditated on his next project. "I nearly didn't wait for you." His hand drifted up to cup the bulge at his crotch.

"But you did wait."

"Lucky you." His gaze was sharp. "What've you done with your tits?"

Emerald looked down at her favorite summer dress, the blue one with the white polka dots. The neckline was low enough to show twin swells and a deep cleft. "Push-up bra," she admitted. "It's new."

"Show me." He thumbed the remote without a glance at it, his attention lazily but entirely devoted to her as the TV went blank. With a naughty smile she stepped in close to him, slipping the tiny buttons down the front of her dress one by one until the golden-brown slopes of her breasts were in full sight, cupped and presented by the lace sling of her bra.

"Pretty," he allowed, moistening his lips. Emerald shimmied a little for him, making her boobs wobble enticingly. "Very... yellow. You got knickers to match?"

"Uh-huh."

"Let's see them."

Obediently she drew up her skirt to expose stocking tops and the triangle of silky material. He smiled. "Like that. You buy them for me?"

Emerald nodded.

"But Max will get a kick out of them too, I bet."

"Mm." That was the thing about this purchase, she thought; she'd be getting double value.

"You know I can hear you two at night? The walls in this place are pretty thin." He savored the way she blushed. "Not that you're exactly quiet. But I hear every thump of the headboard, every little groan and squeal." He caressed the towel-covered knot of his cock, and the bulge twitched visibly. "Drove me nuts for a year, doll."

"I'm sorry." Her voice was husky.

"I can even hear the sound he makes when he slaps your fat ass."

Emerald's eyes widened: Greg's brutal crudity was one of the things that made him so different from Max. He was shamelessly honest, and it was one of the things that made her hot. He liked the fact that she had a big ass, and he told her so. He liked the fact she was a slut, and the more he treated her like one the more she acted that way. "Does it annoy you, hearing us?" she asked. He smirked.

"I just grin and join in for the ride, doll."

"Oh."

"Now show me that big bum of yours."

Turning, Emerald pulled up the back of her skirt. She heard the intake of his breath.

"Oh, *yes*. Like two loaves put out to rise." He'd been a bakery assistant as a student, she recalled: his tales about what had been done to the dough during quiet moments had been enough to put Max off bread for good. She crossed her legs and leaned forward, hands on her thighs, giving him the best possible view. "Fuck, yes," he said in awe as she wiggled her backside. "I want that." He stood, the better to run his hands over her cheeks and down the barely clothed split between them. The elastic was taut across her asshole, the gusset stretched tight over pussy lips that already felt swollen. Greg's fingers crudely but very accurately found the sinkhole of her cunt through the cloth.

"You won't be able to take these back to the shop, doll. They're already wet." Every poke of his fingertips on the sodden cloth exacerbated that situation and Emerald whimpered. There was the sound of a towel hitting the carpet. "You ready for some of this?"

Glancing over her shoulder, Emerald saw the cock she was getting to know so well: heavy, dusky, with a bit of a lean to the right; it stood proudly despite the scrotum beneath that seemed to be trying to drag it down by sheer virtue of its weight. That was the thing about Greg: his dick was good but his balls were something else, and they produced prodigious quantities of come. Emerald was sure they were to blame for the swiftness with which he recovered and was ready for more. Was *she* ready? "Oh, yes."

"Then get down and ask nicely."

Falling to her knees, she shimmied out of her dress and faced the object of her desire, wetting her lips. It swayed a little and Greg stroked it up and down.

"Please," she said sincerely.

"Not good enough, doll."

"Please, sir…" Leaning forward, she delicately tongued those big balls in their velvet pouch.

"Better." His glans was glistening.

"I want it so much." She kissed his bollocks and licked her way up his shaft.

"That's 'cos you're a slut, Emerald," he sighed pleasurably. He was so clean from the shower that he was almost tasteless until she sucked the faintly salty precome from the eye of his cock. Putting her hands on his hairy thighs, she lost herself in the art and pleasure of giving him head. He wrapped his fingers in her hair, guiding her, unhurried. He pushed all the way to the back of her throat and when she took the length without gagging he nearly purred. "Emerald."

She opened her eyes and looked up at him, knees splayed and ass thrust out, her mouth wrapped around his turgid cock.

"I've got a surprise for you." He nodded over her shoulder.

Confused, it took a moment before she broke away and turned. There in the doorway, arms folded, stood Max with a face like stone.

"Shit!" squealed Emerald, clapping her hand over her mouth as if she could hide the fact it had just been pleasuring their flatmate's cock. "Oh, shit! I'm sorry!"

"Yeah," said Max. "You look sorry."

She tried to scramble to her feet but Greg's hand tightened in her hair, shoving her back down; that was such a shock she went momentarily limp. "Oh, no," he said. "Time to face the music, Emerald."

"You knew?" she shrieked.

"Of course he knew." Max came into the room and hunkered down so as to be on eye level with her. "He told me what you two were planning today. He told me everything. What did you expect? He's my mate, isn't he?"

"But he started it!" It sounded childish even as she shouted the words, but she meant it. The furtive affair had begun one evening that summer when she and Greg had been lying out on the roof, in swimwear, listening to their MP3 players. Greg had, without warning and without a word, rolled over and put his hand square on her breast.

"Like you resisted," replied Max.

Emerald gaped. She hadn't resisted. She'd let Greg squeeze her tit and then pull down her bikini top to play with them both, his hand firm and slow. She hadn't struggled or protested or even spoken, pinned to her towel by the sunlight and the glint on his opaque sunglasses, overwhelmed by his assurance. Her nipples had stiffened to his touch and her breasts had heaved to meet him. After ascertaining her response to his tweaking and pinching and kneading, he'd slid his hand down to her sex and explored that, sliding inside her bikini bottoms to find her hot wet softness, her yielding openness. And when she started to tremble and twitch he'd heaved himself on top of her and fucked her, not even bothering to remove her bikini. Then he'd rolled away and gone back to reading his *Mac* magazine, still without a word.

"It...it just happened. I don't know how." After that, it had only taken a possessive slap on her butt as she leaned over the sink to water the plants, or a confident tweak of her nipple as she met him in the corridor, to teach her that her whole body was tuned to his key. She'd waited home one morning, pleading that she had stomach cramps, and then as soon as Max went out to catch the bus she'd gone naked into Greg's room to endure his triumphant smile and submit to his voracious appetite. He'd fucked her on every piece of furniture in the house by now. "It was his idea," she wailed.

"It was your idea, Emerald." Max's eyes were like blue Arctic ice. "I saw the way you looked at him. I knew you wanted to fuck my best mate, no matter how much you denied it. So I told him to make a pass and see how you'd react. I was right, wasn't I?"

"Oh, my god!" Realization came crashing in on her. "You're out of your mind!"

"Really?"

"It's been three months!" she gasped. "You knew all this time?"

He nodded. "I knew. I knew the first time, when you were

all over me that evening, hot and gagging for it like you were in heat. Was it guilt, or are you just a horny little bitch? I knew every single time you fucked him, Emerald, because you were… so different. Pliant and eager. Like he'd greased you up for me. I *knew* all right."

"Shit," she whispered, seeing him in a totally new light, remembering the ferocious intensity of his lovemaking over these past months. She'd been too wrapped up in herself to question it. "Max, this is twisted…"

"Twisted." He smiled sourly. "You betrayed me with my best mate, Emerald. You took something that was ours—mine—and you gave it away. You lied to me. Hey, you're the one who decided one man wasn't enough for your hot little cunt. Well, now you're going to put your money where your mouth is."

"What d'you mean?"

Greg, who'd kept quiet so far, laughed. "You reckon you need two men to satisfy you, doll. Well, this is where we test that out once and for all."

"Oh, Christ!" She twisted, outraged, but Max shoved his hand over her mouth.

"Shut up." He didn't raise his voice, but there were depths of rage in there. Rage, and something else. "You owe me, Emerald. I'm going to take some of it back." With his other hand he undid the buckle of his leather belt and pulled it out through the loops. The cloth hissed. "Turn her. I want her ass."

"All yours," said Greg. He flipped her over to face him and sat himself down on the carpet, back propped against the sofa, and legs spread wide and straight.

"Greg!" protested Emerald weakly, but if Max was merciless she didn't expect any from him. His eyes twinkled.

"Hey; your bottom likes a good spanking. We both know that."

"I don't—"

"Shut up." He pushed her face down into his crotch. "You've made your bed, doll: now lie in it." One hand pressed the back of her neck. Her mouth and nose full of his exuberant hair, his hard cock pressed up against her cheek, Emerald wanted to argue but short of biting him, couldn't. Her head was held firmly almost at floor level but her backside was still up, her bare cheeks spread. And between those cheeks was a molten heat.

"No need to take these off, even," commented Max, folding the belt in his hand and moving right in to kneel between her legs, nudging them even farther apart. He flicked the stretched gusset that lay tight across her asshole, making her jump. "I'm going to, though." He yanked down the panties to midthigh, exposing her gash—then he struck her on the right buttock, stingingly. Emerald squealed, her cry muffled against Greg's groin. She tried to buck away but Max grabbed her pubic mound with his free hand, holding her up and steady for the rain of blows that was to come.

He used the leather end of the belt and only a short length, but there was no escape from the pain he administered. Emerald found that two men were more than capable of pinning her helpless, however much she cried and thrashed. Her ass was soon inflamed with the burning licks of that leather tongue, her body shining with sweat. It was the fact that it was Max doing this to her that was most unbearable though: smart, considerate, tender Max who'd told her only that morning that he loved her. Told her that, even knowing that she was balling his best friend and wet with anticipation for her next fucking.

"Fuck, man," said Greg, appreciatively, "She's glowing like a hotplate."

Max paused and wiped his forehead. His hand was crushing her clit, his thumb sliding around in a swamp of her juices. "Does that hurt?"

"Yes!" she wailed.

"Think how it felt, me knowing you couldn't wait to get home and give this wet pussy to my best friend. You think you've been punished enough?"

"Yes!"

"You think you needed punishing?"

Emerald took a tear-filled breath. "Yes. I'm sorry!"

He dropped the belt and laid a finger on the amber iris between her swollen cheeks, and Emerald felt the involuntary dilation and flex of her muscles. "He even had you in the ass, I hear. Funny that, because when I asked, you always said no."

"I didn't ask," said Greg with a smirk. "I find she responds best to that."

Max's voice dropped. "Time I reclaimed some territory then."

Emerald heard a crinkle and a ripping sound as he extracted a condom packet from his pocket and tore it open with his teeth. Then there was the sound of his fly being opened, an inhalation, a grunt, and then suddenly his blunt glans was pressing at the gate of her upraised ass and demanding entry. There was lubricant on the rubber, which rendered the penetration bearable—but only just. He still burned as he went in. Emerald cried like something being broken.

"You go, man," murmured Greg.

Swiftly Max found his rhythm, his latex-glazed length pistoning in and out of her ass, his hands on her burning butt, his thighs pumping into hers. His scrotum slapped against her reddened skin. "Fuck, yes," he groaned.

"Yes," Emerald echoed, her mouth painting Greg's thigh. Greg leaned forward and grabbed her dangling breasts, scooping the orbs from her bra cups and pinching the nipples unmercifully.

"She's going to come, man," he told Max. "You keep fucking

her dirty ass and the bitch is going to come."

Emerald, drowning in pubic hair, groaned out loud.

"Well, I'm not stopping," Max said through clenched teeth. "She's getting it all."

"You were right," Greg announced, his fingers rolling and twisting her nipples like they were dough. "She is a dirty slut. Your girlfriend is the dirtiest slut I've ever fucked. I want her again when you've finished with her, man."

Max shot his load at that, thrusting deep into Emerald's hot and clenching hole. She came louder than he did, though. When he pulled out and rolled away to skin off his rubber, she collapsed sobbing between Greg's thighs.

"My turn," Greg muttered, rolling her onto her back and kneeling astride her head to stuff his erection between her lips. Her face was burning with exertion and her mouth felt like glue.

"I need a drink!" she begged.

"You're about to get one, doll."

She wrenched her mouth away. "Please!"

"Get her a glass of water," said Max, and when Greg cast him a frown added with steel in his tone: "My rules, mate."

With a grunt Greg dismounted and stomped away into the kitchen. Emerald lay quietly, trying to get her breath back. She could see Max watching her, his expression dark, his hand moving on his cock.

"You like two men then?" he asked, his voice low but not gentle.

"Max, I love you…"

"That's not what I asked."

Greg came back in with a glass of tap water. Max took it from him, helped Emerald sit up then, still supporting her with one arm, and lifted the glass over her face. She looked up at it yearningly as he tilted it near her lips. Very carefully, without letting the glass touch her, he poured the water out in a narrow stream for her to catch in her open mouth. As she gulped some spilled down over her sweat-sticky breasts and her belly, and she was grateful for how cool it was on her skin. Her whipped ass itched like fire on the carpet.

"Put her on the table," said Max as he laid the glass aside. "Face up."

Between the two of them they lifted her and laid her upon the coffee table. It was a good thing it was sturdily built. Emerald was carefully positioned so that her head hung off one end, her throat drawn out long and taut. Max went down to kneel between her thighs again. "Open your mouth for Greg, Emerald," he instructed.

She obeyed and Greg, kneeling, took instant advantage.

"Good girl." His cock was shiny and sleek with frustration; he'd waited longer than he was used to for satisfaction. He dipped into her, painting the inside of her mouth with his salt, then pushed deep down her throat. In this position no bend in her neck impeded him. Emerald's eyes bulged and she squirmed. Hands closed over her ankles.

"Careful," said Max. "She has to breathe, remember."

Greg withdrew, letting her gasp, then slid in again. He was as careful as he could be in the circumstances. As he began to thrust, Emerald felt her legs being lifted and draped over Max's shoulders, felt him slip his still-proud cock into her sex and began to stroke evenly, without urgency, leaning into her thighs and pelvis.

"That's it. That's what you want isn't it, Emerald? Two of us. Fucking your cunt and your mouth at the same time. You want your cunt and your throat both full of cock, spit like a roast pig, you dirty little whore." His hand stroked her mound, avoiding direct contact with her clit but teasing all around it. Emerald could feel the pressure building in her spine and her head. She groaned around Greg's thick shaft. He slapped her right tit till it danced.

"You know what I'm going to do?" Max continued as he eased in and out of her wet slot. "I'm going to give Greg fucking rights to you. What are friends for, after all? You want two of us, Emerald; you've got it. Whenever he likes he can fuck you. When you get home from work, when I'm away, when I'm busy with something on the TV...when I feel like watching. 'Cos you know what? I really enjoy seeing him fuck you. That's so hot, Emerald, the way his big cock stretches your lips and your throat. I can see it going down, girl. I can see how you're getting fucked by him. And I can feel how your cunt's so hot around my prick because you've never had sex this good, you dirty bitch. You think you can cope? Belonging to us both? Serving us both with your sweet snatch whenever we want it?"

Greg's movements were growing jerky and less controlled. His hands bit into her shoulders. Emerald was running short on air, but caring less and less. Her blood was roaring in her ears.

"Pull out!" ordered Max. "Come on her tits—I want to see it—come all over her tits, you bastard!"

With a wrench Greg pulled out of her mouth to reposition himself and with a last manual stroke let loose a gush of come. It didn't fly far; it never did with him. It foamed out like champagne from a bottle, splashing on her breasts and belly. Emerald reached up to suck and lick his balls as he spasmed, but she wasn't allowed to guzzle for long because Max's thrusts became suddenly staccato and then he was coming in her again, for the second time that morning, groaning and cursing. He reached out and wet his fingers in Greg's semen, smearing it over her nipples then bringing it down to where his cock was pulsing and throbbing against her. Fingers slicked with the other man's come, he stirred her clit until she arched and flailed and Greg had to sit on her face to muffle her screams.

Emerald spent the afternoon on the sofa, draped across both their laps and snoozing as the two men raced Formula 1 cars on the games console, equilibrium restored. Every now and then she'd stir and Greg would slap her ass. Between levels Max would stroke her hair and smile, his eyes full of dark, possessive tenderness.

THE LAST CIGARETTE

Heidi Champa

They drove to the party in silence, the cold leather of the BMW feeling good wherever their skin touched it on the warm summer night. It was his father's birthday and they were going to his parents' huge house to celebrate. Once they arrived, he would disappear into the smoky den, to talk politics and finance with his father's rich cronies. She would wander around talking to no one, drinking and sneaking cigarettes on the balcony. Everyone else would smoke in the house, but he disapproved of her smoking, especially in front of his parents.

Out in the night air, she breathed deep the scent of the flowers in their lush garden. She lit her cigarette, letting the smoke fill her tight lungs. She exhaled and looked over the balcony. The railing was wide, and she leaned onto the cold stone, just a bit a first, then farther. This allowed her head to rest beyond the railing's border and her feet to barely reach the concrete below.

She leaned farther over the balcony rail, hesitating for a

moment before lifting off her feet, her hands gripping the edge tightly. The feeling made her tingle with a mixture of fear and excitement. Leaning just a bit farther, she dangled her head, feet off the ground, the cigarette falling into the shrubs below.

"What are you doing?" She heard the voice behind her, making her head snap up and landing her feet back on the floor.

"Nothing." Looking at him in the dim light, she saw his tell-tale black vest, signifying that he was a waiter. His hand moved to his mouth, as he inhaled his own cigarette.

"Shouldn't you be inside? Don't you have to mingle, or something?"

"What about you, don't you have a job to do tonight?"

"I just needed a break; I wasn't expecting company out here."

"Sorry to disappoint you."

"Oh, you haven't." He inhaled deeply and blew smoke in her direction. She stepped closer still, noticing his broad shoulders, his large hands.

"I've seen you here before, you know, at other parties."

"Funny, I don't remember seeing you. I must not be spending enough time out here. Who are you hiding from anyway, your husband?"

"Fiancé."

"Oh, sorry." He smirked in the dark. "He must be a real catch."

"Well, no, but he's rich."

He cracked a smile, and laughed at her admission.

"I can't believe I said that. I shouldn't have said that."

"Why not?"

"Because it's terrible."

"I don't know, not if it's true. Is it?"

She didn't know how to answer. He took another drag of his

cigarette. He looked at her expectantly.

"So, does he know what you do out here?"

"I don't think he cares what I do out here. I could do anything."

"Really, is that a fact?"

"Yes, it is."

"Interesting."

He just stood there, staring at her. At that moment, she felt her face go hot, and he took a step closer to her. He closed the small gap between them, eyeing her up and down, holding a cigarette between his fingers. She took it without thinking, and he raised a lighter toward her. She guided his hand gently with hers, and deeply inhaled. Just touching him caused an electric current to run through her. It felt foreign and strange after months of dormancy. He stood just a bit too close, waiting for her to retreat. She didn't. Their combined smoke pooled around them, as the sounds from inside faded and grew. She thought of asking his name but didn't really care. He didn't ask for hers.

The next few moments ticked by at a snail's pace. She waited for him to nudge them over the edge. Behind them, she heard the first words of "Happy Birthday to You" echoing through the room. She knew she should go inside, do the right thing. But as she turned, he grabbed her wrist.

He pulled her against him, his fingers digging slightly into her back. Their faces almost touched, and she was unsure of what to do next. Making up her mind for her, he kissed her, plunging his tongue into her mouth. It felt more right than anything had in months, maybe years. His teeth caught her bottom lip, and he tugged gently before covering her mouth again. His fingers traced down her neck to her collarbone, darting under the fabric of her dress. Pressing her against the facade of the house, he ran his hands into her bra, pinching her nipples between his fingers. His breath tasted of smoke and scotch, just like her fiancé's would after a long night in the den. But somehow, this was different. Giving herself over to the moment, she realized she wanted more. She freed her mouth from his and tasted his neck with her tongue, biting the soft flesh between her teeth.

He reached down and lifted the hem of her skirt. He slid her panties down to her knees, and she moaned as his fingers touched her softly between her legs. He smiled when he found her wet and her own heat overwhelmed her. It was as if he had unlocked her cage and set her free. He held her and continued stroking, her hips bucking along with his rhythm. The balcony door was open, but she didn't bother to muffle her cries of pleasure. She almost willed someone to come out on the balcony and find her. She whimpered when he removed his hand from her moist pussy. He put his two wet fingers up to her lips, and she stuck out her tongue to taste herself on his skin. Her fingers pulled at his zipper, as if they were controlled by someone else.

Turning her around, he pushed her onto the balcony's cool stone rail. He nudged her forward until her head hung heavy at the edge. She was barely standing. He knelt down behind her and ran his tongue over her wet lips, spreading her wide with his long fingers. He teased her clit with his fingertip, as he speared her pussy with his tongue. She looked down over the edge and allowed his mouth to devour her, until she felt her knees begin to weaken. Before she lost her footing, he stood up, and grabbed her by both hips, rubbing the tip of his cock over her wetness.

Entering her gently at first, his teasing strokes caused her to push back against him, her cunt anxious for him. But soon he was pounding harder, deeper. He grabbed both of her hands roughly, and pulled them behind her back. His hips surged her body forward on the balcony rail, and her feet came off the ground, high heels dangling from her toes. Her hands were tense in his hands; she gripped on to him furiously. Her fear started battling her pleasure for her brain's attention. He pushed into her deeper, her body moving farther over the rail. As he swirled his hips, her pussy swallowed him hungrily. She wanted more of him, but she couldn't move. He had her suspended. He fucked her slower, slower, easing himself and her forward inch by inch. Her body felt out of control, his cock barely leaving her cunt before plunging back inside.

Slowly, he pulled his cock from inside her pussy and she felt his grip loosen on her hands. She clawed at him, digging her nails into his soft flesh. He seemed to be letting go. Just as the thought crashed through her mind, he pumped his cock inside her again and again, and her hands slipped a little. Her thighs tightened, trying to keep her steady. A scream started to form in her throat. She teetered on the brink, staring down into the darkness below, paralyzed. Seconds passed by slowly, as she felt herself inching toward the ground. Suddenly, he pulled her back hard onto his cock, releasing her hands, and her toes touched cool cement. Pleasure ripped through her, and his hand clamped over her mouth to keep her quiet. She rode back against him, the waves of ecstasy and adrenalin rushing together like a tide. Shuddering, she felt the convulsions deep inside her pussy. Biting into his palm, she shook and rocked as he violently fucked her through her orgasm. He had started her revolution, her liberation. She felt him slow down his pace. His cock tightened, and with one last push, he broke, shooting cum deep inside her. Slowly, she realized she was back on the balcony, her shoes by her feet, her body safely where it belonged.

Straightening up, she felt her heart pound in her chest. She heard his zipper and she turned and saw him walk back into the party. She had not felt this much of anything in so long. Her panties lay next to her feet, and she looked at them for a long minute. Lighting another cigarette, she glanced at them one last time before turning and walking off the balcony.

SOME LIKE
IT HOT

Alison Tyler

You get heat in the summertime. You get heat in front of a blazing fire. You get heat when the furnace breaks with the knob stuck in the ON position. And you get heat when the two boys you're dating show up at the same time, and in the same place.

Although not the type of inferno you might expect.

Because first there was Jarred, with his tousled good looks, and his full-lipped mouth—a Cupid's mouth, a *girl's* mouth. When we met, he gazed at me as if I'd answered every dream, every prayer, every fantasy he'd ever had since the time he was fourteen years old. How could I turn down a look so sweet? How could I deny the request in his gray-blue eyes, the destiny he said that only I could fulfill?

And then there was Marlon, with his dark hair, and his black eyes, and the way he confessed the mind games he played on the girls he dated, making me think that I was different. Making me feel like a partner in crime. Marlon's specialty was twisting

and turning every subtle emotion until he got what he wanted.
His looks didn't hurt, either. Ever embracing the dark, he made
a uniform out of black jeans, black jackets, black long-sleeved
shirts still hot from the iron.

Some, as they say, like it hot.

I was dating the good boy. The blond boy. The light boy.

But I craved the dark one. The bad boy. The sly fox with the
handcuff key on his key ring and the coal in his soul. I knew I
oughtn't. I knew I really shouldn't. But I did. Simultaneously.
One in the daytime and one at night. One on the surface and
one under the covers. One in the church pew and one in the
back alley.

God help me, I dated them both.

Jarred said he could marry me. He said he could love me. He
said we might one day be that handsome old couple you see on
Hallmark cards, holding hands at their children's graduations,
engagements, weddings.

Marlon said he could fuck me six times before sunrise.

God help me, I did them both.

But I'm getting ahead of myself.

Siouxsie and the Banshees were popular when I was in college.
My roommate knew all of their songs. I knew "Peek-a-Boo."
Rebecca took photos for a living, working endlessly, ravenously,
to get her name in print. I was a student, and I would have been
a starving student if I hadn't subsidized my coed lifestyle with
two different part-time jobs. Three days a week, I worked at a
clothing store in West L.A. Nights, I popped corn at an art house
movie theater near La Brea, two blocks from Melrose.

"Peek-a-Boo" played at both locations, in the hip clothing
store and in the velvety scarlet lobby of the movie theater. "Peek-
a-Boo" was my mantra. I played peek-a-boo with my bangs,

looking out at people from under my glossy midnight fringe. I played peek-a-boo with my boyfriend, Jarred, seeing him every weekend while sleeping with the projectionist, Marlon, during the nights.

Rebecca didn't approve. She liked Jarred and thought that if I wasn't going to be faithful to him, at least I should be honest. I was twenty-one, and to me, honesty was honestly overrated.

"Just tell him," she insisted. "Tell him that you want to see other people."

"I'm not *seeing* other people," I corrected her.

"That's right. You're just fucking them." She gave a grim smile as she inserted a fresh roll of film into her Nikon. "You know, you're playing with fire."

"Some like it hot," I'd respond, as flippantly as I could.

After each one of these fights, I'd leave the apartment, heading to work, trying to figure out why she cared. She wasn't my mother, for god's sake. She was my roommate. At the time, I felt as if I were playing a game: balancing both men, expecting nothing but pleasure, dark pleasure at the sensation of fucking Marlon one night, then sliding into Jarred's bed the next morning, playing peek-a-boo with my emotions. I knew plenty of men who behaved like this.

Why shouldn't I?

"Because it's dishonest," Rebecca said one evening, stopping by the theater to get a free box of popcorn. "Jarred thinks you're his steady. Don't you see that you're going to get burned?"

I shrugged. Rebecca didn't date. She lived behind her camera lens, taking pictures and making judgments. And if that was enough for her, then I wished her well. But I needed more in my world. I needed Marlon to fuck me while patrons watched *Sid and Nancy* or *Last Tango in Paris*, or any one of the many mostly depressing second-run movies we played. Then, I needed

Jarred to take me again, in the morning, when we were fresh faced and Ivory scented and ready for Sunday brunch and walks in Griffith Park.

I wanted different things from my different men. Couldn't Rebecca understand that? Marlon was all rock and roll—in his dyed black jeans and his tight T-shirt, he looked like the celebrity musician he hoped someday to be.

Jarred's clothes were interchangeable. He had dialed into the khakis and blue work shirt uniform of the serious graduate student. One day, he'd trade up to suits. The differences ran far beyond the way my men dressed to the way my men fucked. Or didn't fuck. Marlon fucked. He fucked me hard, the film making a whirring sound behind us, sawdust on the floor of the projection room. He'd make me suck his cock—I say "make," but I would have done so anyway. Yet I liked the way he pushed me to my knees, laddering my hose, slapping my face so that I'd open my mouth wider, wider still.

"Come on, girl. Take it. You can do better than that. Suck it like you're hungry."

He'd use his cock to slap my cheeks. He'd face-fuck me, gripping on to my hair and driving his cock home. I'd be breathless, tears in my eyes, when he'd pull me to standing, rip my panties to one side, and fuck me lubed up only with my own spit. But I didn't need lube. The foreplay—oh, what an innocent word for the degrading preshow he'd unveil—would be enough to get me juicy.

He'd slam into my pussy, talking to me the whole time about how, during the next reel, he was going to take my ass.

Jarred didn't even say "fuck," he'd trained himself so well. He might say "damn" when something didn't go his way. But he had a G-rated vocabulary. You never knew who might be listening. That was his policy.

I should have made that policy my own.

Because someone was listening. And doing more than listening. Someone was watching.

Jarred and I made love. That was what he called it. "Do you want to make love?" he'd ask, soft and sweet, his mint-fresh breath on my neck.

Marlon didn't make love. And he didn't ask. He just took. Pushing me up against the wall, biting my shoulder. Hurting me with the power behind his thrusts. He fucked me all over the theater: In his projection room. In the ladies' restroom. Behind the popcorn counter. In the alley in back of the theater. He didn't care. I found his attitude addictive, because all Jarred did was care.

"Did I leave enough tip?" he'd ask after dinner. "Did you want to go to the beach this weekend?" he'd say, checking in with me. "Did you get enough to eat?"

I don't think Marlon cared if I put anything in my mouth aside from his dick. He wasn't about my needs. He was all about his. And his needs were all about his cock.

But, god, what a cock.

He was built slim, streamlined, that rock-and-roll god physique. Nicotine-stained fingers. Well-worn Docs. Ageless and graceful. He had long hair that fell in his eyes. Tattoos that crawled up his skin. A cigarette and Jack Daniels habit that devoured a chunk of his paltry projectionist income. I knew better than Marlon. I mean, I knew better than to want him, knew I was supposed to want Jarred.

And that made me want Marlon even more.

Jarred was the light to Marlon's inky blackness. When I looked at Jarred, I saw a future…a future something. Something big: Bank president. Mayor. Executive. But I was scared that he was *my* future, and I didn't like the thought of it.

Then I looked at Marlon, and I saw no future all, and somehow that was scarier still.

* * *

"Jarred called," Rebecca would say, taunting me some days, hating me for having two men when she had none.

"What'd you tell him?"

"That you were sleeping."

"Thanks," I said, grinning at her, surprised that she'd lied for me.

"Sleeping with Marlon," she added and I turned on my heel, hoping she was kidding.

"Just tell him." Her huge blue eyes even wider as she imposed not-so-silent judgment.

I didn't want to. If I didn't have Jarred, then fucking Marlon wouldn't seem so...so what? So dangerous? So necessary. It would just be fucking. Any hoodlum in L.A. could have played the same part. It was the difference between the two men that mattered.

To me, anyway.

"You're playing with fire," Rebecca snarled at me, but I shut out her voice, ignoring the warning tone. I should have paid more attention. I should have seen the sparks start to flare.

On Valentine's Day, Jarred wanted to see me.

"I'm working until one A.M.," I reminded him, thinking of my plan to wear no panties under my dress, to flash Marlon when he came down the stairs. We were playing a romantic double-feature for once: *Some Like It Hot* and *Casablanca*. We could listen to the actors on screen, while he fucked me behind the counter.

"I've got a surprise for you," Jarred told me on the phone. He'd called the theater directly. This was pre–cell phone. Pre-Twitter. Pre-Tumblr. It was easier to get away with all the traditional antics of unfaithfulness. But fire is as old as man. I should have counted the matches in my box.

"I'll stop by after work," I promised, liking that thought even more, going to the trouble of tucking a fresh pair of knickers into my purse—because Jarred wouldn't understand the concept of going commando.

Unfortunately, on this day for lovers, Marlon had a plan of his own. And his plan involved the new ticket taker, a buxom redhead named Lynette, who somehow managed to make room for Marlon between her legs in the tiny booth at the front of the theater. She tore tickets for customers, while he ate her out, and I did my best not to burn my hand on the popcorn maker.

I couldn't believe he'd fuck another girl so close to me that I could almost smell her pussy. I couldn't believe he'd put that look in another girl's eyes, knowing that when he was finished, he'd have to walk right by my counter, his mouth wet from her wetness.

My stomach lurched. The scent of popcorn made me nauseous, but I plastered a smile on my face, and served up the clients.

Thank god, for Jarred. I thought. *Jarred loves me.*

From my spot behind the counter, I could see Lynette squirming, and I realized Marlon's magic tongue had just made her come. He waited a moment, choosing the perfect time to slip out of the ticket booth, not clocked by anyone but me as he slipped up the stairs to start the movie.

Anger, bitter and hot, bubbled in me like the butter in the popcorn maker. Once the last viewer had walked through the swinging doors, I dug my panties from my bag and put them on behind the counter. My breath was coming faster. Silver dots flashed in my vision. I was surprised when Jarred showed up at the theater. He spoke through the hole in the glass to Lynette, and she waved him through without a ticket. I started to smile for real, feeling suddenly grateful to Jarred. Sweet Jarred, with

his neatly pressed khakis and his wallet full of unwrinkled bills.
But then I noticed the look on his face.

He wasn't holding flowers, or a Valentine card. He was
holding a proof sheet. *Rebecca*, I thought, as he said the word,
as he passed the eight-by-twelve shiny piece of paper over to me,
letting me see the individual squares of Marlon fucking me in
the alley.

Jarred stared at me, then looked at the photo sheet in his
hands. He shook his head in disgust, before turning and walking
away, ending the game of peek-a-boo in a heartbeat. I gazed
out the window and saw Rebecca waiting for him, camera on a
strap around her neck.

Fuck all. She'd told me to tell him. But not because of any
moral attitude. She'd wanted him herself.

I glanced back down at the proof sheet. The last shot was
different from the rest: Rebecca and Jarred, fucking on my bed.
So he did have it in him. She'd been the one to show him how to
rub two sticks together.

A rushing sound filled in my head. The sound of Malibu
when it burned. I swallowed hard. I blinked to clear my eyes.
Above the white noise, I could hear Marlon fucking Lynette on
the stairs as Marilyn Monroe cooed for Tony Curtis.

Some like it hot.

I'd always put myself in that group. But now I had no
boyfriend. No roommate. I turned off the popcorn maker and
walked around the side of the counter. No job.

A man standing near the door reached into his pocket for a
pack of cigarettes. "No smoking in the lobby," I said, pointing
to the sign over the door before walking outside and into the
ashes of my life.

FIREBOY

Christopher Tolian

Hop hop hop into the fire. Burn baby-o! Burn all gorgeous indigo neon white. Consumed subsumed burned through to ash devoured by eternity spit out those lush luscious lips and born again to fall and fall and fall through everything to lie weeping panting hurt a beautiful pain blazing red brilliance. Glory be to the bebop father who blew his wad of creation between the smooth smooth thighs of the mother of forever. Screaming out the top of my head blinded deaf dumb numb, take it all on faith. I strike the match and smile.

Whiskey chokes. Nicotine smoke burns. Eyes water, mixing with the sweat coating my face. Sirens wail in the distance, barely heard over the industrial music pouring out under harsh bebop trumpet lines. I whirl and collide with a torch. Lunge and grab. Flame licks my face, evaporating the perspiration. I laugh and light another cigarette.

Curtains fly apart, catching me off guard. Deep red frames

dark dark blues. Weak spotlight falls on a shadow center stage. Static filtered through to distortion blasts from the speakers. "Fireboy!"

A cheer goes up from near the stage. I'm pushed forward, dragging the torch with me. I focus on the figure. Small, heroin sleek. Shaved head. Eyes closed. Push in closer. Young, looking all jailbait taboo. Muscles sinewy and hard. Baggy pants ride low, barely hiding slowly gyrating hips. *Fireboy's a girl.* I laugh. Small breasts pulled tight and flat, pierced nipples straining at the bandage across her chest. Pockmarks, tiny burns cover her cheeks, the rest of her face porcelain perfect. Arched, flagrant painted eyebrows, like miniature tribal work.

Music starts in. Slow, heavy groove pulses under distorted bass. Eyes open and she looks around, catching me with a grin. "Got a light?" Words all soft and muted drawl. A pearl glistens in her tongue. She holds out two torches of her own. I tilt the flame in. Kerosene and clove, heavy smell of potential. *Whoosh pop!* Fire catches hold and crackles.

Flames jump and she winks through the heat, eyelashes curling back from those flashing deep greens. She is a troubadour of fire. An earth poet leaping and spinning through the conflagration.

A body presses against me, all whiskey and sweat and wild wild eyes. "Watch out, boy! What you got inside all bundled tight, it'll burn, baby. Just like the whole world's burnin' tonight." Voice drops to a messiah whisper, rushed and harsh, dragging my attention to him. "Gonna catch fire and light up from the inside out. And that fireboy? Well, she got the match now." He laughs a deep rumble. "How 'bout a little fast-forward? And, baby?" His grin goes mile wide. "Watch the hurricane."

Jump the jive with a little too much heat. Let go of the torch and stand transfixed. Fireboy flips and spins, fire wrapping her.

She breathes it and throws it out over our heads. Arcs convulse around her and she screams a wild scream that's answered by the crowd. Feel the sound ripped from my throat as she calls the flames to her.

A gust of wind blasts across the room. Lights go out like firecrackers. *Whoosh bang.* Music echoes into silence. Fireboy jumps offstage laughing. Pale smoke follows her breath. She grabs my hand and pulls me hard toward the door, through the sudden noise of a hundred people running, voices rising in a wave that washes over me. Like the rain slamming through the door.

Out into the crazy mix of the city. They say a hurricane is blowing in. Yet the music floods out most every gaudy, shining door. Out into the street and through it all I'm dragged pulled under by fireboy. She is her own force of nature. Larger than her tiny body. A comet blasting through everything, carrying me in her wake.

Bricks crack under our feet. Whole damn city's coming down in the smoke as lights fade and fireboy burns brighter. Screaming to shake the world loose to go spinning off into heaven or hell. Raging on 'cause it can't go back. Sirens and fire and cars careening past through air trying to drown us. All shot through with redemption missed.

She turns her head as we stumble through the river washing over the road. Eyes flash and she smirks, sparks lighting off. "Greasy black clouds piss off the sun so he hides his light now. Stars don't come round here no more neither. Everything gettin' all hot 'n' close 'n' all I can see 'n' smell 'n' taste is you, baby."

Breath like kerosene and lit cigarette. Righteous desperation. "Breathe deep, baby. You won't never get used to it." Her eyes shine back at me and everything else just kinda slips past and away till none of it matters. Nihilistic epiphany, all incandescent and numb. "Don't think you ever want to. 'Cause you have no idea. Not a fuckin' clue."

I try to answer. Wind whips up, stealing thoughts. Can't feel the rain for all the flames. Blazing fire tornadoes we whirl under the spinning clouds. A boarded window crashes as we fly through, engulfing someone else's life, their artifacts, with our smoldering steps. Slam onto a bed, sheets smoking as we fall, pulling off soaked clothes. I unwind the bandage from her chest. This woman...no, girl. This girl trying to be a boy. Becoming more than either. I look at her and see red and orange and golds that god wouldn't believe. But I feel her. Heat outlines sinewy muscles. I trace her ribs as sweat crackles, throwing up a steaming aura. The rings piercing her nipples burn moon scars into my fingers. Lips meet and the roof ignites, flying off into the storm.

Naked, exposed, and glorious beneath screaming angels and boiling clouds.

"Burn me, baby." Her voice is quiet, hiding under the roar of wind. "Catch me up and consume me.... I'll be the kerosene, you the match. Burn with me, baby-o." She looks down at me, stroking and caressing as all around the world ends. Tattoos glow fluorescent under her skin. Blacklit swirls and jagged lines that dance and gyrate as she moves over me. My hands burn, lighting off flames across her hips, her breasts as I pull her hard onto me. My skin is ash devoured by her kerosene tongue. Eyes blaze like the Fourth of July and I take her in. That part of her that's stronger than me. I let it have me as I take her body with mine. Sit up and break her against me. Tongue and lips blister with her heat. Mouths hunger, biting and feral. The pearl breaks. Cracks against the heat in my mouth. I am a fire-eater.

Tingle across my skin. Shiver. Pale heat builds and spreads. A spark, like a switch. Engulfing. Tension breaks and the world explodes in Technicolor bliss. Scalded. We swirl all neon, angle up into the dark sky. Kerosene slips through to musk and sweat and the singed smell of her. Like vanilla and burned almonds. Bitter and enticing.

Sound concusses a pounding rhythm that drags me round and round till I lose the ground, body combusting and I hang on to her, bury myself as I burn from the inside out 'cause I'm made of kindling. Those little bits and pieces of life that lie forgotten till the match is struck. Fireboy laughs and prays and burns bright as me. Scream out hallelujah as the hurricane tries to touch us through the flames. I burn and burn and let her smother me so I don't blow away as everything goes. I gather her ashes to mine and swallow them into myself.

Fall back into her and open an eye.

She smirks, flames dancing in those green eyes, burnishing them gold. "Got a light, baby-o?"

Fucking fireboy. Strike a match and laugh.

JUST ADD WATER

M. Murphy

Jason came home to find me installing a brand-new shower curtain.

"What are you doing, Naomi?" he asked. I'm generally not a domestic goddess. The only screwdriver that ever finds it's way to *my* hand is the one made with vodka and tonic. So I could tell from the tone of his voice that he was a bit confused, although I didn't turn around to check out his expression.

"What does it look like?" I asked coyly as I slipped another hook into place.

"I mean, *why* are you doing that? What was wrong with the old curtain?"

"The old one was black," I said, sighing with relief as I fastened the last of the silver hooks onto the shower bar, and then pushed a strand of my long dark hair out of my face.

"And black is out?" he asked, sounding more muddled than before. I work in fashion, and I'm often spouting phrases like that to him: *Brown is the new black. High heels are the new little black dress*. But this particular change in scenery had nothing to do with the whims of the decorating gods. *This* was all about sex.

I turned to look at him now, smiling as I walked to his side. Without a word, I began unbuttoning his shirt.

"Are you taking *this* off because this is black?" he asked next, his blue-gray eyes bright. Clearly, he could tell something was up—I was undressing him after all—he simply had no idea what that something was.

"I changed the shower curtain because I wanted one I could see through," I explained without pausing in my mission to make him naked. "I'm taking off your shirt because I want you to try out the shower."

"The shower's the same," he said smugly. "It's only the curtain that's changed."

"That's true," I nodded, now working on the button fly of his faded jeans. "But I want you to take a shower anyway. Because now I can watch."

I had gotten his fly undone, and at my words, I could feel his cock hardening through the fabric of his boxers. Jason knows full well that watching turns me on like nothing else. Early on in our relationship, I confessed exactly how much of a voyeur I am: how my heart beats faster when I see a couple kissing, how even the mere sight of a man slipping a hand down a woman's arm can make me wet.

"Tell me more," he had said softly when I first told him. We were sitting at a little sidewalk café, and he'd leaned in over the table to whisper, "I want to know *why* watching makes you wet."

"It's just so sexy," I'd replied, speaking in an equally low voice, embarrassment at my confession turning my cheeks the color of the raspberry sorbet in my bowl. "You know, witnessing even the most subtle erotic connections. It makes me feel as if I'm part of the action."

"But how can you be part of the action?" Jason had asked. "You're just watching."

"Yeah," I'd agreed. "But I imagine."

"You mean you *fantasize*."

"Except, it's not just fantasizing," I had tried to explain. "Because I've seen part of it. With my own eyes. I just extend the vision."

"With that dirty imagination of yours." Jason had grinned, suddenly understanding. My filthy mind is one of the things that he loves best about me.

What I'd never told him was that watching him take a shower was my number one voyeuristic fantasy. Every morning, when he disappeared behind that black shower curtain, I would stay in the bed, wrapped in our warm sheets, thinking about him under the shower spray. It was all I could do not to rush into the bathroom and fling back the curtain to watch. The thought of my strong, muscular man lathering himself up, running the bar of soap across his broad chest, then down his flat stomach, and lower to his...

"Watch?" he asked now, interrupting me from my decadent daydreams. "You're going to watch me take a shower?"

"Oh, yes," I told him, the plan continuing in my head, although I didn't speak the words aloud: *I'm going to watch you take a shower. And I'm going to pretend you don't know I'm here. And I'm going to touch myself.*

I wouldn't have to fantasize any longer. As long as he left the door open, I could gaze directly from our bed to the shower, because the curtain I'd bought was entirely sheer, like Saran Wrap. When I'd first spied the curtain at the store, I had started to tremble, knowing instantly what I was going to do, what this shower curtain would mean to me, to Jason, to our sex lives. How funny that something purchased from the hardware department could manage to turn me on more than any sex toy ever could.

"Are you serious?" he asked next, his voice hoarse, and I nodded hungrily. But because I couldn't resist seeing my man in need, I dropped to my knees and nuzzled his cock through his boxers. He groaned and became momentarily silent, as if afraid that saying a single word would break the magic spell—the spell that had potentially won him a postwork blow job. But then, when he saw I wasn't getting up from my position, he helped me, sliding down his boxers and jeans, releasing his hard-on.

I took a second to admire his stunning cock—because it *is* a thing of beauty—and then I parted my lips and drew the head into my mouth. Jason sighed and thrust forward, but I put my hands on his thighs, keeping him in position, wanting to set the pace myself. Gently, I bobbed my head up and down, slicking him up, getting him wet.

From this position, I could glance to the left and see the two of us reflected in the mirrors that line one wall of the bathroom. Even watching *myself* turns me on, so I kept my eyes open as I worked Jason, reveling in the taste of his skin, in the way he moved his body, craving the connection of my mouth on his rod.

I was wearing my version of Ms. Fix-It clothes, shorty overalls over a tight-fitting white tank top, my long dark hair up in a ponytail. Jason had his head back, his longish red hair falling away from his face. I liked the way I looked sucking Jason's cock while he stood there with his shirt off and his jeans opened, liked the way his expression was one of total ecstasy.

Jason, who doesn't share my fixation for watching, had his eyes closed. He groaned and arched his hips, lost for a moment in the pleasure before apparently remembering that I had just told him something he found confusing, something completely unexpected. He opened his eyes and looked down at me, then ran his fingers through my hair, unclipping the silver barrette that held my ponytail in place so that my hair fell long and free down my back. Then he drew in his breath and asked, "That's the only reason why you got a new curtain? So you could watch me?"

"You're quick," I said, wrapping my fist around his rod and jacking him for several strokes. He had to lean back against the lip of the sink to steady himself, and I could tell that if I changed my fantasies, if I told him I just wanted him to fuck me, right then, right there, he wouldn't have said no. He would have taken me on all fours on our fluffy black-and-white bath mat, or maybe bent me over the edge of the porcelain sink and fucked me from behind. But I'd spent hours in preparation for this moment. I'd bought the curtain, fiddled with those damn hooks, set the whole scenario into motion. Now, with the help of a little hot water, Jason was going to make my desires come true.

"You don't mind, do you?" I asked, suddenly feeling nervous. What if he said he didn't *want* to be watched? Or worse, what if he made fun of my fantasy?

"No," he shook his head quickly. "I don't mind at all." I could tell what he was thinking. If I'd been ready to blow him just at the thought of *watching* him shower, what might I be willing to do for him if he did what I asked?

"But what's your part in all this?" he wondered. "Are you going to be naked, Naomi? Are you going to join me?" He seemed to like that thought. His cock throbbed in my fist.

"You'll see when the time is ready," I told him mysteriously. And then I left him alone, stepping into our bedroom and sprawling out on the bed. My legs were shaking, and my heart was pounding so loud I was sure Jason could hear the steady throbbing beat. I'd been waiting for this moment for so long, and now, finally, everything was in place.

Hungrily, I faced the bathroom and watched—watched Jason. He seemed to be extremely aware of my eyes on him. He added a little something extra to every action: a little bump and grind as he kicked out of his jeans, a little extra move to his hips. I laughed out loud as I watched him turn on the water and adjust the temperature, moving with such exaggerated gestures, waggling his hips in a sexy little shimmy. He was even singing that old Rockwell song, "Somebody's Watching Me." But then I stopped laughing and just stared as he slid his blue-and-gold boxers down his sturdy thighs and then stepped out of them.

Jesus, now I could see his ass. His beautiful taut ass, made luscious from hours cycling on the weekends. It was all I could do not to hurry back to his side, to offer to help him with the soap. Oh, lord, I could picture that so easily: running the soap down his back, over his buttocks, down his thighs...

Wait, I told myself. *Just wait. You've been daydreaming about this for so long. Don't rush.*

Waiting may be the hardest part, but I was sure this time it would be worth it.

For months now, I'd thought of this precise moment. Ever since we'd first moved in together. My fantasies had taken over from the second when he pushed the curtain aside, stepped into the bath, and flipped the handle to switch the water from tub to shower. I'd touched myself while lost in this vision, running my fingertips along my pussy lips: pinching my clit, fantasizing about the exact second when I would be able to watch. And that second was finally here.

The shower curtain worked perfectly. It was as if I were

looking through a window—nothing to hide Jason from my prying eyes.

Unable to stop myself, I had to unfasten my overalls and slip them off. Once I was down to my tank top and knickers, I reached down and stroked myself through my satiny panties. Simply brushing my fingertips over my clit made me moan.

Jason closed his eyes as soon as the spray hit him. I knew that the water must have felt delicious, caressing his body after his hard day at work. But I didn't really care how *he* was feeling. I was consumed instead by my own fantasy—fantasy turned reality—watching my boyfriend as he turned slowly under the shower, as the water beat down on him. Oh, he looked so damn hot with the water cascading over his muscles, his fine abs, his fantastic thighs. He was a wet dream turned real.

But I wanted more.

Use the fucking soap! I wanted to catcall, yet I bit my lip instead and let him go at his own pace. Who was this tramp with the filthy mind and dirty mouth? Who was this girl with her hand inside in her pale pink panties, thrusting two fingers into her own dripping wet pussy? God, it was me. Look at what I'd become. No, that's not right. This is who I'd *always* been. Only now, thankfully, I had free rein to let myself revel in my darkest desires. And that's why the voice in my head was screaming out directions as if I were Martin Scorsese instead of Naomi Rogers.

In truth, Jason didn't need my help.

He would know what to do, was in tune with my needs. He understood full well that this was more than just your average clean-yourself-quickly shower. This was masturbation fodder. This was foreplay like nobody's business.

After he'd rotated under the spray for several minutes, he finally reached for the soap.

Yes! I wanted to yell. *Yes! Finally. Soap!*

But I kept to myself, watching fiercely, drinking in every movement.

I will readily admit that I may be the first woman in the history of the world who got wet installing a shower curtain. But there you go. All afternoon I had been growing more and more aroused. Now, I was on the very cusp of coming with hardly any stimulation at all.

Once more, I tried to tell myself to be patient, to enjoy the masterpiece in front of me. I'd worked for this. I ought to savor every second—god, every *sexy* second—as Jason continued to lather up his amazing physique. It was exactly as good as I'd imagined. In fact, this was better: the way he rubbed his hands over his body, the way he soaped himself, slowly, sensuously.

So that's how he does it, I thought. *He takes his time.*

It was as if he were talking to me with the movements of his hands; as if he were telling me to mimic his own motions. I took my hand out of my panties. Then slowly, I touched myself, echoing his gestures. I ran my hands over my breasts through my T-shirt, pausing to tweak my nipples through the thin white fabric. I stroked my fingertips over my ribs. I caressed my own slim thighs.

But when Jason started to touch his cock, I couldn't handle it.

"Oh, fuck," I muttered to myself. For one last second, I tried to stave off the need to climax. But I just couldn't. Watching Jason stroke his cock under that heady spray of water was too much. I pulled my panties off and started to rub my clit in quick circles. When he jerked his cock, I tripped my fingers across my clit. When he started to move his hand faster, so did I. He seemed to have forgotten that I was watching. He was no longer putting on an act, he was taking care of his own needs. This turned me on like nothing else, and a shudder ran through me.

As I circled my clit with my fingertips once more, I felt myself start to come.

I was surprised by the intensity of the climax. The power of the pleasure made me moan out loud, but Jason didn't even look in my direction. I guess that he couldn't hear me while under the spray of the water. Or maybe he heard me but didn't think he ought to look my way. Maybe he understood exactly how important it was for him to stay focused simply on bathing; to pretend that I wasn't there, wasn't anywhere near him; to be solely consumed by his own needs:

The soap. The water.

My body behind him.

"I was wondering when you were going to join me," he said, smiling as I pulled back the curtain and stepped inside. I was still trembling from the power of the climax. Watching him wash himself had brought me such intense satisfaction, yet I managed to find my voice, to put a bit of strength behind my words.

"You're a tease," I told him, taking the soap away.

"What do you mean? You wanted to watch. I gave you something to look at."

"But you knew I'd want to join you. You knew if you started touching yourself I'd need to take over." I ran the bar of soap between my hands, making bubbles, and then set the bar in the soap dish and reached for his hard cock. "Here," I said proving my point, "let me help."

No, Jason doesn't have the same sort of voyeurism fixation that I do. But I saw his eyes widen as I began to stroke him, spreading the lather over his shaft, using the soap to lube my fist as I jacked him once more.

What he does like to watch is how big his cock looks in my small fist. And he likes it even more when I work him firmly, powerfully, as if that cock were my own. I did that now, gripping him exactly how he likes, hitting just the right rhythm, until he sighed and closed his eyes, leaning back against the cobalt blue tiled wall for support. I worked him for several moments before grabbing the shower nozzle off the wall and spraying the soap away. Then I slid it back into place and went down on my knees.

The water rained down on me as I gave my man the second half of the blow job I'd begun earlier. Jason groaned louder than he had before, as if being in the shower released some of his inhibitions. He gave himself over to the way my mouth felt on his cock, the way the water rained down on us both, the warmth and the heat of the shower. Until suddenly he couldn't wait any longer. He moved back and pulled me up, standing me under the spray and moving to take his position behind me. I put my palms flat on the tiled wall and held myself steady. And as he started to fuck me, as he thrust his cock inside me, I realized that I was on the verge of coming again, coming so soon that I couldn't believe it.

"You liked watching?" Jason murmured.

"Yeah."

"What did you like?"

He wanted me to talk: to describe the experience, how I'd felt. But I was having a difficult time even breathing. How could I eloquently explain what the sensation of watching him shower did to me? I couldn't. Yet, Jason wouldn't let up.

"Tell me, Naomi," he insisted. "What did you like about it?"

"Just seeing you," I managed to whisper. "Just seeing you touch yourself. As if you were all alone. As if you didn't know I was there. Do you always jack off in the shower?"

"Not always," he said. "Sometimes."

"You looked so sexy," I continued. "God, Jason, you looked amazing."

"It was the thought of you watching," he confessed, surprising me. "That turned me on like nothing else."

I sucked in my breath when he said that. I couldn't believe the words. I had been sure he would *let* me watch, because he knows how much I like to look. But I hadn't realized that being watched would be a turn-on for him. Weren't we well matched? Knowing that he'd found being watched exciting brought fresh fantasies instantly to my mind. What other scenarios might we explore in the future...?

"You like it when I fuck you like this?" he asked next, bringing my attention back to what we were doing now: what he was doing to me with his cock.

"Oh, yes," I told him. "Just like this."

He kept talking to me like that while he fucked me, and then he reached down between my legs and stroked my clit, sending me spiraling out on fresh waves of pleasure, coming so hard that if Jason hadn't gripped on to me to hold me steady, I would have slid back down to my knees in the tub and let the water wash me away.

He came a moment after, hard enough to make me groan with him, and then he turned me around beneath the shower spray, so that I was facing him, so that I could look into his beautiful blue eyes and see the light dancing there.

"Was that what you wanted?" he asked me in a low tone. "Was *that* what you've been fantasizing about?"

I nodded, my wet hair falling forward, so that he brushed it off my face in order to stare into my eyes.

"Instant pleasure," I grinned at him, still breathing hard. "Just add water."

ABOUT THE AUTHORS

JANINE ASHBLESS is a full-time writer living in the U.K. Her short stories for Cleis have previously appeared in *I Is for Indecent, Frenzy,* and *Best Women's Erotica 2009.* She has written three erotic novels for Black Lace and two collections of short stories, specializing in paranormal and mythical themes: the latest collection, *Dark Enchantment,* was published in January 2009. Her website is www.janineashbless.com and she blogs at www.janineashbless.blogspot.com.

HEIDI CHAMPA is a typical last-born child. Snarky, attention-seeking, and rebellious, she chooses to write dirty stories to keep herself out of real trouble. Her work appears in the anthologies *Tasting Him: Oral Sex Stories* and *Frenzy: 60 Stories of Sudden Sex.* She has also steamed up the pages of *Bust Magazine.* If you prefer your erotica in electronic form, she can be found at Clean Sheets, Oysters and Chocolate, and The Erotic Woman. In addition to her flare with the written word, she knows every last sentence of the movie *Clue* by heart. When she's not writing, she can be found reading or filling her iPod with more music. She lives in Pennsylvania with her husband. Her greatest wish is that sarcasm would translate better in the written form. Find her online at heidichampa.blogspot.com and myspace.com/heidi-champa.

ANDREA DALE's stories have appeared in *Afternoon Delight, Frenzy, The Mammoth Book of the Kama Sutra*, and *Dirty Girls,* among many others. With coauthors, she has sold novels to Cheek Books (*A Little Night Music,* Sarah Dale) and Black Lace Books (*Cat Scratch Fever,* Sophie Mouette) and even more short stories. She thinks the best laid plans should always include getting laid. Her website is at www.cyvarwydd.com.

BELLA DEAN is new to the business of dirty stories. She still blushes when she types but has no plans to give it up. She lives with her small family in her small house in her small town. She stopped playing with matches ages ago. Mostly.

JEREMY EDWARDS has been frequently published online (at Clean Sheets and many other sites), and his work has appeared in more than twenty-five anthologies offered by Cleis Press, Xcite Books, and other print publishers. Drop in on him unannounced (and thereby catch him in his underwear) at http://jerotic.blogspot.com.

A. D. R. FORTE's erotic short fiction appears in various anthologies including *Best Women's Erotica 2008, Yes Ma'am*, and *Hurts So Good* from Cleis Press. Her stories have also been featured in several Black Lace *Wicked Words* collections.

Like Andromeda, the chained lady of the stars, **SHANNA GERMAIN** works best when chained to something hard and wet. Her award-winning work has been widely published in places like *Best American Erotica, Best Bondage Erotica, Best Gay Romance, Best Lesbian Erotica*, and more. Visit her online at www.shannagermain.com.

P. S. HAVEN was raised on comic books, *Star Wars*, and his dad's *Playboy* collection, all of which he still enjoys to this day. His work has been published in the *International Journal of Erotica*, the *Best American Erotica* series, and *B Is for Bondage*. His writings can also be found on the Internet at scarletletters. com, cleansheets.com, and ruthiesclub.com. P. S. Haven peddles his smut from Winston-Salem, North Carolina, where he fights a never-ending battle for truth, justice, and the American Way. More at www.pshaven.com.

MICHAEL HEMMINGSON lives in Southern California where he writes screenplays, smut, and systematic sociological intro-spection (the three *S*'s) about simpaticos, sluts, and significant others (the other three *S*'s). He's been burned and played with fire too much, too often, so that he has some wisdom, but is generally stupid and keeps repeating his mistakes when it comes to sense and sensuality. His academic study of strippers and the self, *Zona Norte: An Auto/ethnography of Desire and Addiction,* was recently published by Cambridge Scholars. His collection of literary stories, *Pictures of Houses with Water Damage,* is forth-coming from Black Lawrence Press. His first feature film, *The Watermelon,* is making the rounds of the film festival circuit.

JOLENE HUI (www.jolenehui.com) is a writer of literary and erotic fiction and about anything else her fingers feel like typing.

She's been known to write a horror column for *The Flesh Farm* and a hockey column for *Inside Hockey*. One of Tonto Books's first authors, her literary fiction has been published in their *Tonto Short Stories*, *Tonto Christmas Stories*, and *More Tonto Short Stories* anthologies. She's also been published by a variety of newspapers, magazines, websites, Cleis Press, Pretty Things Press, and Alyson Books. She still holds on to her dream that she will one day be the mother of a standard poodle and frequently daydreams about cheesecake. She is based in Los Angeles.

NIKKI MAGENNIS lives in Scotland and writes erotica. You can find her work in many anthologies and the occasional jazz mag. Her second novel, *The New Rakes*, is out in January. Read more at nikkimagennis.blogspot.com.

SOMMER MARSDEN's work has appeared in numerous anthologies. Some of her favorites include *I Is for Indecent, J Is for Jealousy, L Is for Leather, Spank Me, Tie Me Up, Whip Me, Ultimate Lesbian Erotica '08, Love at First Sting, Open for Business, Tasting Her, Hurt So Good*, and *Yes, Sir*. Sommer is the author of novellas for eXcessica, Whiskey Creek Press Torrid, and Eternal Press. She has many addictions and has no intentions of getting help for any of them. They currently include merlot, writing smut, long walks, the downward dog position, biscotti, and red candles. You can visit her at SmutGirl.blogspot.com to keep up with her dirty ramblings.

N. T. MORLEY is the author of sixteen published novels of erotic dominance and submission, including *The Parlor, The Limousine, The Circle, The Appointment, The Visitor, The Nightclub*, and the trilogies *The Library, The Office*, and *The Castle*. Morley can be found online at www.ntmorley.com.

M. MURPHY lives in Alaska. For half the year, she doesn't remember how to sleep. But she makes it up during the other half. Her work has appeared on several websites and in several *Penthouse* publications.

A fan of "big weather," **TERESA NOELLE ROBERTS** has happily traded the glorious thunderstorms of her native Finger Lakes to enjoy choppy surf and nor'easters in Massachusetts. Her erotica appears in more anthologies than you can shake a dildo at, including *Hurts So Good: Unrestrained Erotica, The Mammoth Book of the Kama Sutra, Cowboy Lover, Succulent,* and *Frenzy.* She's also the author of *Rain at Midsummer, Lady Sun Has Risen, Pirate's Booty,* and several other erotic romances published by Phaze Books.

The author of more than two hundred published short stories, **THOMAS S. ROCHE** writes fraudulent mythological metafictions, slapstick romances, and neofabulist smut. His ten books include four volumes of horror/fantasy, three volumes of erotic crime-noir, and three volumes of erotica. He works a day job at porn producer Kink.com and teaches sex education at San Francisco Sex Information (www.sfsi.org). He also blogs about cryptozoology, particle physics, and brain-eating zombies with utter credulousness at www.thomasroche.com, and twitters with moderate enthusiasm at www.twitter.com/thomasroche. He is currently at work on a novel about mutant subterranean robots that devour human souls through the esoteric use of blowfish spines.

CHRISTOPHER TOLIAN spends his days climbing windmills in the cornfields of central Illinois. Nights are spent raising gypsy girls where the sidewalks end and dancing with his beautiful muse outside the city lights of Chicago. He has been published in the online magazines Clean Sheets, Slow Trains, Scorched Earth, and Divine Animal (R.I.P.) To paraphrase a dead man, "I write for the angels and the madmen." Please send comments, cigarettes, and whiskey to bastinado75@gmail.com.

SOPHIA VALENTI likes lurking in shadows and learning sultry secrets. She prefers hot summer nights over crisp fall days and fire-engine red lipstick over pretty pink gloss. She is on good terms with old flames but is always looking for someone new to spark her interest.

I. K. VELASCO is a Filipino-Canadian living in Dixieland. By day, she reaps Corporate America's bounties so she can pay her bills. By evening, she seeks her true nature through writing. She also cooks for her loved ones, strums enough cover songs on guitar to entertain at parties, and plays with her kittens.

J. D. WATERS lives on the East Coast. He likes steak over fowl, red wine over white, blondes over brunettes, and whips over paddles. He recently quit smoking, but he can't get rid of his BiC.

KRISTINA WRIGHT's steamy erotic fiction has appeared in more than sixty anthologies, including *Bedding Down: A Collection of Winter Erotica; Dirty Girls: Erotica for Women;* and four editions of *The Mammoth Book of Best New Erotica.* While she will only confess to being a good girl who writes bad, she loves creating characters that flirt with the dangerous side of love and sex. Visit her at www.kristinawright.com for more not-so-naughty confessions about the life of an erotica writer.

ABOUT
THE EDITOR

Called a "trollop with a laptop" by *East Bay Express,* a "literary siren" by *Good Vibrations,* and "overcaffeinated" by her favorite local barista, **ALISON TYLER** has made being naughty a full-time job. Her sultry short stories have appeared in more than eighty anthologies including *Rubber Sex* (Cleis), *Dirty Girls* (Seal Press), and *Sex for America* (Harper Perennial). She is the author of more than twenty-five erotic novels, most recently *Melt with You* (Virgin), and the editor of more than forty-five explicit anthologies, including *J Is for Jealousy* (Cleis), *Naughty Fairy Tales from A to Z* (Plume), and *Naked Erotica* (Pretty Things Press).

Ms. Tyler is loyal to coffee (black), lipstick (red), and tequila (straight). She has tattoos, but no piercings; a wicked tongue, but a quick smile; and bittersweet memories, but no regrets. She believes it won't rain if she doesn't bring an umbrella, prefers hot and dry to cold and wet, and loves to spout her favorite motto: "You can sleep when you're dead." She chooses Led Zeppelin over the Beatles, the Cure over the Smiths, and the Stones over everyone—yet although she appreciates good rock, she has a pitiful weakness for '80s hair bands.

In all things important, she remains faithful to her partner of nearly fifteen years, but she still can't choose just one perfume.

Find her on the Web 24/7 at www.alisontyler.com, or visit www.myspace.com/alisontyler if you want to be her friend.